"I'VE SEEN YOU AROUND, AND YOU know, in this liberated age, a woman doesn't have to just wait for—"

"Where?"

"Pardon me?"

"*Where* have you seen me around, sweet-cakes?"

She glided over the question as smoothly as twelve-year-old Scotch. "Simon," she said softly, mildly rebuking. Her voice stirred masculine nerve endings all over his body.

"I do have a name, you know, Simon." On the last word her voice dropped to a caressing murmur. "And it's not *sweetcakes*."

"Oh? And what is it? Since you seem to have a pretty good grasp of mine."

She smiled and prevaricated. "Yes . . . Simon Faro. Very . . . Egyptian. And I'm . . . Cleopatra."

"Cleopatra?"

"O'Nile."

"Cleopatra O'Nile," Simon said, trying it out. "And—let me guess—you've come all the way here to . . . kiss my asp?"

"Oh, that's only the tip of the pyramid, Simon."

WHAT ARE *LOVESWEPT* ROMANCES?

They are stories of true romance and touching emotion. We believe those two very important ingredients are constants in our highly sensual and very believable stories in the LOVESWEPT line. Our goal is to give you, the reader, stories of consistently high quality that may sometimes make you laugh, sometimes make you cry, but are always fresh and creative and contain many delightful surprises within their pages.

Most romance fans read an enormous number of books. Those they truly love, they keep. Others may be traded with friends and soon forgotten. We hope that each LOVESWEPT romance will be a treasure—a "keeper." We will always try to publish

**LOVE STORIES YOU'LL NEVER FORGET
BY AUTHORS YOU'LL ALWAYS REMEMBER**

The Editors

UNDER
THE
COVERS

LINDA
WARREN

BANTAM BOOKS
NEW YORK · TORONTO · LONDON · SYDNEY · AUCKLAND

UNDER THE COVERS

A Bantam Book / March 1996

ISBN 0-553-44514-6

Published simultaneously in the United States and Canada

PRINTED IN THE UNITED STATES OF AMERICA

OPM   0 9 8 7 6 5 4 3 2 1

ONE

Simon Andrew Faro had committed seventeen sins in the past six hours, by Jo O'Neal's tabulations. Unfortunately, not one of them was a bookable offense.

She'd tailed him halfway across Saratoga Springs, she was hungry, disgruntled, out of chocolate bars, and had already clocked in six hours of department time, but she'd seen no evidence whatsoever that he was involved in a crime.

It didn't seem likely that he was about to commit one in the Temple Bell Sushi Bar either.

Jo glanced covertly around the crowded restaurant from the corner booth she'd taken opposite the back room, where the click of pool balls accompanied the grunge rock on the jukebox. The atmosphere was as raw as the fish, which, contrary to what the casual tourist might guess, had been rated the best in town by local sushi fans. Apparently not everyone objected to the pool-hall atmosphere and the cadre of local teenage dropouts in the back room. The owner, she knew, had a record as long as a pool cue and had learned to cook—or not to, as the case may be—when he was in jail. She presumed he was now capitalizing on his varied experience.

Faro wasn't hard to spot. Even in the eclectic surroundings he stood out. Lounging at a small table with his long legs stretched out in front of him, he wore a scarred leather bomber jacket that hung open, displaying three state-of-the-art cellular phones stuck on his belt. His hair was just a little too long to be acceptable in polite company, and he had a small stud in one ear.

A bookie, the chief had told her, along with several unrepeatable adjectives. Ever since Faro published an article that criticized the Saratoga Police Department and the superintendent, in particular, known to everyone as the chief—getting Simon Andrew Faro had become some kind of a personal vendetta for her boss. He claimed Slippery Si was hiding his criminal activities behind the guise of being a writer. Jo had the feeling that maybe the criminal activities were a cover for the writing instead of the other way around. She knew he'd done some time, but after looking over the case, and his activities since, his six months in prison seemed more like a research project than a penchant for crime. But the chief had obviously not wanted to argue the finer points. "I want you to drag him in here by his little magna cum laude pin" was the way he'd put it.

Unfortunately, as far as Jo had been able to tell, there was no magna cum laude pin in evidence, unless that was what he was wearing as an earring.

It was possible, Jo worried, that he'd spotted her, that he knew he was being followed and had deliberately played it straight all day. It was even possible, in the worst-case scenario, that he was innocent.

The idea gave her immediate heartburn accompanied by a vivid image of the chief reacting to a report of Faro's innocence. She picked up a chopstick from the caddy on the table and tapped it with distracted frustration against the table, listening to her stomach rumble and watching Faro eat his lunch.

Real men, apparently, did indeed eat sushi, at least in places like this one.

Not just the polite nibble either. He was wolfing down raw fish, wielding his chopsticks like a samurai, looking not in the least like he was concerned with running a betting ring or doing anything else she could arrest him for.

"Sake." The waitress appeared at her table with a porcelain jug and a tiny cup, which she set in front of Jo.

Jo frowned at her. "I didn't order sake."

"From Mr. Si," the waitress murmured, nodding toward Faro's table.

Startled, Jo dropped her chopstick and flicked her suddenly panicked gaze toward Faro. *Had* he spotted her? For most of the morning she'd been so far behind him, she couldn't even spot him!

But he was staring straight back at her, his gray eyes steady, memorizing her facial features, one corner of his mouth lifted in an amused, make-your-own-rules grin that was sexy enough to add to her sudden panic a small, involuntary shiver that made her throat go dry.

His eyes moved, briefly, to her mouth,

to the tiny cup of sake she'd gripped in her nerveless fingers, then back to her eyes. He lifted his own sake cup, smiled a little more, and said something she couldn't hear. She didn't have to. She could read his lips. "Bottoms up."

It was some sort of unspecified elemental challenge, and it wasn't covered in the police manual on undercover work. Not *that* kind of undercover work anyway.

He was a *bookie*, Jo reminded herself. A criminal. A *petty* criminal at that.

But there was nothing remotely petty about the man toasting her with a sake cup. The man was a biological imperative. A bookie? She couldn't see it. Piracy on the high seas, maybe.

When she made no move to take a drink, he gave a barely perceptible shrug and raised his own sake cup to his mouth, then slowly lowered it, his steady, impossibly gray Cool-Hand-Luke eyes riveted on hers. A wash of something that was a cross between outrage and illicit ecstasy trickled over Jo's nerve endings.

Any doubts she'd had about his guilt vanished like smoke in a Saratoga breeze. Any man who packed that much potency into a single toast shouldn't be loose on the streets.

A minor scuffle just inside the front lobby caught a shred of Jo's attention. One of the teenage hoodlums who claimed this particular block as his territory was making his way toward the poolroom, and on his way had picked up an unclaimed carafe of sake and was about to chug it. A waitress was striding toward him, looking determined.

To Jo's surprise, Simon got there first. He commandeered the little jug and handed the kid a can of soda, then deftly caught a pocket calculator that was slipping out of the back pocket of the kid's baggy pants and placed the little machine in the teenager's free hand. The waitress hovered uncertainly, foiled by Simon Faro's panache. The teenager guzzled the soda with panache-in-training. A clucking pigeon hovered at the door, attracted by the trail of cracked corn dribbling from the kid's back pocket.

Jo watched, mesmerized. How did Faro know the kid? Why was he showing concern for the kid's drinking habits and his pocket calculator? Unless . . . the obvious conclusion hit Jo like a sandbag full of outrage. He *was* a bookie. Was he taking bets from teenagers? Fleecing street kids for whatever spare change they'd scrounged?

As a crime, it wasn't much, but as an affront to law-enforcement sensibilities, Simon Faro's arrogant, outrageous flouting of the law was a gauntlet that had just been thrown down smack in front of Jo's feet. He was *asking* to be caught, dammit! He was committing a crime he knew she'd witness, and planning to get away with it. Well, he was wrong. If Simon Faro took one teeny, weeny little bet from the soda-swigging kid, Jo was going to arrest him, read him his rights, and haul him downtown in handcuffs.

She scrambled out of the booth and made her way toward the cashier, where she could settle her nonexistent bill and listen to the conversational exchange between Simon and the kid.

It was exactly what she wanted to hear.

"So who do you think, Nickel?" Simon was saying.

"Who do I think?" The kid belched in a gentlemanly manner. He was good-looking in an alternative rock sort of way, and a gleam of obvious intelligence belied the pigeon-feeding persona. He gazed reflectively at the soda can and gave the matter some thought. "You got change for a fifty?" he asked finally.

"Unh-unh," Faro said without looking at his wallet. "But maybe I will next time I see you."

He turned and headed out the door, neatly sidestepping a few more pigeons loitering at the entrance to the lobby.

Jo's gaze followed the broad shoulders, trim hips, long, muscular legs, and easy gait. Picturing him with his hands cuffed behind his back brought a vague, inexplicable twinge of regret, but any regret she felt faded when the kid known as Nickel turned and tossed out a handful of corn, and a flock of pigeons as thick as a Golden Gate fog descended, squawking and babbling, on the unexpected bounty.

When the feathers cleared, Simon Faro was nowhere to be seen. Nickel ambled toward the poolroom, having finished with the soda. And Jo realized with abrupt and horrible insight that *change for a fifty* probably had nothing to do with change for a fifty.

The crime had already been committed, and she'd missed it. What was worse, Faro had vanished. Vamoosed, in the four seconds that she'd been mobbed by pigeons.

Cursing under her breath, Jo set off across the lawn toward where she'd seen him last at a dead run.

So who the hell was she?

Simon Faro leaned one shoulder against the doorway support and watched his shadow go sprinting by him with a look on her face that combined equal parts disbelief and determination. He imagined it would turn to sheer jaw-clenching outrage when she realized she must have outdistanced him. He was beginning to read her pretty well.

Reading her, as a matter of fact, had added one of the few interesting notes to an otherwise information-free morning. He'd given her fifteen minutes, tops, before she lost him.

He'd been wrong. This was one lady who didn't give up on what she wanted. He'd ditched her twice already—once in the library, between the 850's and 931's, and then again with an unsignaled exit on the crosstown expressway—but she'd surprised the socks off him by strolling into the Temple Bell five minutes after he'd started his lunch.

He'd even considered, briefly, that it was a coincidence, that she hadn't been tailing him and he didn't have to put her in the category of dangerous potentials, but his instinct for self-preservation was a little too well-honed for the assumption.

Too bad, in a way, Simon concluded, bending forward at the waist to aim a look toward her retreating backside. He liked the way she moved. The lady with the holes in her Reeboks offered a pretty appealing view from the rear. Nothing overtly sexy. She hadn't gone to any trouble to emphasize her feminine attributes. Her haircut—straight across at chin level—looked like a home job with an oversized pair of sewing scissors, and the closest she'd gotten to makeup was a sunburn across her chin and the tip of her nose. Still, she had a way of getting the job done that inspired . . . imagination. He could picture her as the kind of woman who told a man what she wanted up front, and stood by her guns until she got it—and then stood by her man when he needed her.

He pushed himself away from the tree and shoved his hands into his pockets, his jaw clamped shut while he watched her disappear around the tulip gardens, then he frowned, considering.

She had to be a local doing low-budget PI work for the bookie he was trying to track down, and the fact was that she'd had a hell of a lot more success in tailing him than he'd had in locating the bookie, who was supposedly using the Temple Bell as headquarters.

Usually he could get a lead on who was having him tailed by checking out the talent. Employers, criminals included, tended to gravitate toward PIs with the reassuring appearances and attitudes they had themselves.

None of his colleagues, present or past, however, looked like a cross between Bambi and Oliver Twist. Or was not-so-coincidentally nimble enough to keep up with Simon Faro.

The thought made him frown a little more. Surveillance at Simon's level was more than a matter of basic skill and clever scoping out. It was a psychological game played between tail and mark, and with rare exceptions the game went to the best player. There was only one conclusion to be drawn in this case.

He must be letting her win.

He grinned. That had to be it. Subconsciously, he didn't want to lose her. As a matter of fact, he'd actually been enjoying the game.

But the fact remained that he needed a tail like he needed an extra hole in his wallet. Having more or less ditched her, it only made sense for him to complete the job.

His health club was half a block away, and conveniently applianced with massage facilities. Also conveniently segregated by sexes. Not the way he wanted to spend his life, but there were times it was appropriate.

His erstwhile tail, whether or not she chose to emphasize her feminine attributes, was in no way going to pass for a man.

Fifteen minutes later Jo pushed open the scarred wooden door of the Bayview Health Club, walked into the lobby, and hid behind a fake potted fern, a discreet distance from the Formica counter where the receptionist was checking membership cards. She stood where she was, catching her breath and getting her bearings.

She hadn't actually *seen* Simon Faro enter the Bayview Health Club, but she'd tailed him there by process of elimination, sheer luck, and some odd sixth sense she seemed to be developing about the way his mind worked.

The Bayview had started out as a training gym for wannabe middleweight boxers and had progressed over the years of social enlightenment to a training gym for wannabe middleweight boxers that also offered post-workout massages to throbbing heavy-metal music in the physical therapy wing.

Women, the Bayview had apparently decided, had physical needs too. They needed to be masseuses.

It figured that the hedonistic, not to mention sexist, Bayview was the health club of choice to Simon Faro. She should have guessed it. She had guessed it, actually.

Guessed it right. She knew he was there. His car—a little vintage Jaguar that exuded bachelor—was tucked behind the service entrance in a way that made her think he'd spent plenty of time in the Bayview's parking lot. The man himself, Jo was sure, was on the other side of that plywood partition. For one thing, she could hear his cellular phones ringing over the muted vibrations of the music—two of them at once.

Eight and ten rings later, respectively, Faro's phones quit ringing. What kind of a bookie didn't answer his phones? And more to the point, how was she going to find out?

She glanced casually toward the desk clerk, a statuesque redhead in biking shorts and tank top chosen, Jo decided, to accentuate her body-by-Nautilus muscles. In case any casual observer missed the point, she had on her arm a tattoo of a dragon whose tail twitched every time her biceps bulged. It looked like she'd been hired for her heavyweight-contender qualities rather than her powers of observation, but even so, she was bound to notice the slightly disheveled woman in baggy chinos and nylon jacket hiding behind the fake fern sooner or later.

Furthermore, if Faro slipped out the back without her noticing, he'd be long gone before Jo made it to her car.

When Faro's third phone started ringing behind the closed door, Jo rolled her eyes heavenward, counting, but this one, to her surprise, he picked up immediately. She took a step closer to the partition, put her ear to the plywood, and heard, just barely, his brisk, businesslike, "Faro here."

The voice softened almost immediately to a personal tone, directed at someone called Melissa. Jo pressed her ear a little more firmly to the wall. It wasn't high-tech surveillance, and probably wouldn't have had the approval of the Bayview's patrons, but it got the job done. Faro's caller had him sounding alternately aggravated, conciliatory, and defensive, probably with good reason, Jo decided.

He muttered something exasperated about buying herself a new coat, said abruptly, "I'm not free tonight," and broke the connection. Jo could almost hear the click of the phone being hung up in the hapless Melissa's ear.

Faro was probably smiling behind the cedar-and-smoked-glass wall. He'd ditched two women in twenty minutes.

A muscle tightened in Jo's jaw.

A blond twenty-something in a purple spandex unitard and enough makeup to carry her safely through an opening at the Met breezed into the lobby and trotted past the desk. The tattooed receptionist glanced up at her. "Room five's waiting for you, Jocelyn. Been here fifteen minutes."

"All right, all right," the blonde answered, heading for the locker room. "Tell him I'll be right in."

Jo didn't stop to consider the unexpected opportunity. She dredged up more of her newly awakened instincts and took it.

"Oh—hi there," she called. The purple-spandexed masseuse squinted at her, and Jo hurried across the lobby, gushing as she moved. She wasn't—normally—given to either gushing or outrageous ploys, but there was something about the image of Simon Faro grinning smugly at his three phones that prompted her action. She was *not* going to be ditched by a man on a massage table!

"*So* glad I caught up with you!" she improvised. "I wasn't sure I was going to be able to make it. And then when you weren't here, I thought—" She reached the door to the locker rooms as the woman was opening it and slipped inside ahead of her. "Well, you can just imagine . . ."

"Excuse me, but—" The frown deepened, emphasized by blue mascara and matching eyebrow pencil.

Jo gave her a bright smile and kept walking. The blonde followed her into the locker room, let the door swing shut, and finished, "—do I know you?"

"Actually . . ." Jo considered the range of answers and settled on "No."

"I didn't think so." The woman fished a hairbrush out of her bag, flicked it through her blond mane, and arranged an artful ponytail at the top of her head. Her bluemascaraed gaze met Jo's in the mirror. "So . . . you lookin' for your boyfriend?"

The thought hadn't previously occurred to her, but she recognized a useful fiction when she heard it. Jo nodded. "Uh-huh."

"He's in there?" One spandexed shoulder lifted in the direction of the massage rooms.

"Yes. He is."

The blue-eyebrowed frown deepened. "What room's he in?"

"Not five, if that's what you're asking. He just got here a couple of minutes ago."

"I don't think there are any other appointments," the woman said doubtfully. "Maybe he's swimming."

"Not unless he swims with his phones. Of course, that's possible."

The blue-penciled frown turned skeptical, and the masseuse dropped her hairbrush back into her purse. "I guess you're on your own, honey. I've got to go."

Jo watched her disappear through a swinging door marked MASSAGE.

"On your own, honey," she muttered to her reflection in the wall-sized mirror behind the counter. Now, where had she heard that before? There must be something in her particular countenance that elicited the sentiment. She seemed to inspire it lately, in everyone from blue-eyebrowed masseuses to police chiefs.

. . . To her ex-fiancé, who, although he'd put it differently, had done essentially the same thing six months before.

Ditched her.

Jo drew in a breath, chewed on her lower lip, and looked herself in the eye. What she'd done, *on her own, honey*, was go out and earn her detective's shield. She was, as her ex-fiancé had been fond of reminding her—with increasing sarcasm toward the end—a first-rate cop.

She wasn't about to lose her hard-won reputation in the chief's account book by letting Simon Faro waltz out of the massage room and disappear whenever he decided it was time to ditch another troublesome female.

Jo hauled her oversized shoulder bag onto the counter and yanked it open. She'd brought along a range of necessities, including a clean T-shirt and change of underwear, but nothing that would do for the job at hand. A quick check of the locker room, however, revealed a well-stocked lost-and-found bin outside the shower room. Someone had left a black spandex bathing suit. It was cut high enough in the back and low enough in the front so that she had to turn it around a couple of times to determine which side was which. Worn over tights and T-shirt, it was a passable facsimile of exercise gear, if one wasn't too picky.

And the client would be positioned facedown, with his eyes closed.

Her search through her bag for makeup turned up not much; she'd used her mascara wand to unclog her bathroom sink two weeks earlier. She put on lipstick—an unlikely shade of burgundy that had been kicking around in her bag for months—and added a couple of artistic smudges across her cheekbones, then teased her hair into the kind of windblown look that seemed to be favored at the Bayview.

Two and a half minutes after she'd fished the lost bathing suit out of the bin, she stepped back to survey the whole effect.

It wasn't bad, she had to admit. In fact, it was surprisingly tacky in a Bayview sort of way. The undersized tank suit had nestled itself into her rear cleavage and pushed the T-shirt up on her chest so that it was slipping off one shoulder. She raised her eyebrows and blinked a couple of times. It just might, for a limited engagement, and in a certain atmosphere, be in the same league as a massage-table Mack the Knife.

She grabbed her bag, reached up to yank the T-shirt the rest of the way off her shoulder, and pushed through the swinging door to confront Simon Faro.

TWO

Some questions were best left unanswered, Simon figured.

Even if they were being asked by a hot little number in skimpy exercise togs and teased hair.

Oh, my, why do you still have your pants on? was one of those questions. Nonetheless, a couple of interesting replies ran through Simon Faro's mind in the few seconds that passed before he recognized her. After that, his answer was a simple four-letter word.

He had the impression that it shocked her, but she didn't miss more than half a beat before she gave him a bright come-hither smile and bounced back. "Oh, my, no. Not without the preliminaries. As a matter of fact, the . . . ah . . . preliminaries are what I'm here for. I'm your masseuse."

"Sweetcakes," he said with equal parts skepticism and disbelieving amusement, "I didn't order any services, preliminary or otherwise, and whoever the hell you are, you're not my masseuse."

She shrugged, a gesture out of character with the sexy getup and the husky catch in her voice, then dropped her oversized bag on the floor beside her, raised her chin, and said, "I am now."

Simon gave the bag an assessing glance, then transferred his gaze to the woman. "Good thing you didn't drop it on your foot. What do you have in there?"

"I like to be prepared."

"Right. With . . . massage equipment."

She shrugged again. The T-shirt shifted. The minimal-coverage exercise getup she wore over the T-shirt wouldn't have moved short of being peeled off—a thought that, considering the way it fit her, raised interesting possibilities. "Right," she said, ". . . massage equipment."

He would have bet six month's phone bills she didn't have the haziest idea of what might constitute "massage equipment," but she was putting up a good front, though a delicate flush was rising to her face.

Curious, he met her gaze and held it, the way he had over sake in the Temple Bell.

She stopped breathing, a process pretty noticeable in the revealing leotard, then her breath caught with a sexy, almost inaudible sound.

For a few seconds Simon forgot what they'd been talking about. Something about taking his pants off.

His own breath escaped in a huff of laughter edged with disbelief. "Sweetcakes, you're either the most responsive woman I ever laid out five bucks for, or you're very good at your job."

Her color deepened to an overtly responsive shade of rose. "Five bucks?" she said.

"For the sake. It seemed appropriate. I've never been followed by any woman quite so . . . adhesive. That's a compliment," he added. "I'd include the qualifying adverbs, but they'd be X-rated on several counts."

"Actually," she said in that husky, breathless voice, "I *have* been following you, trying to catch up with you. Well, here, I have, haven't I? So I guess I'm in luck, because I was . . . ah . . . hoping we could get to know each other. I've seen you around, and you know, in this liberated age, a woman doesn't have to just wait for—"

"Where?"

"Pardon me?"

"*Where* have you seen me around, sweetcakes?"

She glided over the question as smoothly as twelve-year-old Scotch. "Simon," she said softly, mildly rebuking. Her voice stirred masculine nerve endings all over his body.

"I do have a name, you know, Simon." On the last word her voice dropped to a caressing murmur. "And it's not Sweetcakes."

"Oh? And what is it? Since you seem to have a pretty good grasp of mine."

She smiled and prevaricated. "Yes . . . Simon Faro. Very . . . Egyptian. And I'm . . . Cleopatra."

"Cleopatra?"

"O'Nile."

"Cleopatra O'Nile," Simon said, trying it out. "And—let me guess—you've come all the way here to . . . kiss my asp?"

"Oh, that's only the tip of the pyramid, Simon."

His mouth curved involuntarily, half in

response to professional admiration for her bluff, half out of a certain intense and definitely unprofessional curiosity about how far she was willing to take it.

Probably not to a mutually satisfying finale, he concluded. Despite that sexy catch in her voice, she hadn't tailed him over seventeen miles of expressway, sixteen city blocks and a park, and into his private health club to get into his jeans.

"And *where* is it you've seen me?"

"Here, actually. At the gym."

"At the boxing gym?"

"Yes—the boxing gym. And you looked so . . ."

"So irresistible in gloves and a rubber mouthpiece?"

"Right."

"And without my pants."

"Ah . . . yes." She smiled.

That smile had an effect, he had to admit. Or maybe it was the spandex.

"So let me get this straight," he said. "You caught sight of me pounding a punching bag to a pulp, it was love at first sight—with the man, not the bag—you've followed me all morning, and now you're here because you have an uncontrollable urge to . . . give me a massage."

"I guess you've got the story. Close enough anyway," she said obliquely.

Simon's mouth curved a little more at the muttered qualification. Close enough for what? Considering that he could make her blush just by looking at her, he'd bet Ms. O'Nile wasn't in the business of physical services, no matter what her nom de masseuse was. Regrettable, but it didn't change the basic situation. She was working for someone. *Who* was the central question. He could ask politely, or he could push the issue and see how much it took to get her flustered and talkative.

He slid off the table, stood up, and reached for the snap of his jeans.

She went completely still, her gaze riveted on the front of his pants. When he unzipped, she raised her eyes to his face in a hurry.

"Let me . . . ah . . . take those for you," she murmured.

Smiling slightly, he pushed his jeans down, stepped out of them, and handed them to her. He was down to his underwear, and she wasn't going to back off—at least not yet. Not his Cleo.

He moved his hands again, pushing down the shorts. Her eyes didn't stray from his face, though her hands clenched into fists. "Why don't you just . . . get under the drapery there on the table? Just make yourself comfortable while I . . . see about massage necessities."

He got back on the table and reached for the cotton blanket. "Front or back?" he asked with absolute innocence.

"Front or . . ." Her voice had gone a little more husky, and at the last unspoken word it trailed off altogether. Then she cleared her throat and said quite clearly, "Bottoms up, I think."

He stretched out on his stomach and rested his cheek on his crossed forearms, listening to the faintly challenging tone in her voice with satisfaction. She took her time dropping his pants onto the chair, and, he thought with amusement, plotting her next move. "Ready when you are, Cleo," he murmured.

"Right." Simon didn't twitch so much as a muscle when she approached the table, then reached across him, let out a shaky breath, and brushed the tips of her fingers along his shoulders. The light, tentative, inexplicably erotic touch sent messages through every masculine nerve ending in his body. It was probably a good thing, he decided, that he was lying on his stomach.

Her fingertips inched their way down his spine, stopped at the cloth over his lower back, and brushed up again.

He could feel the trembling in her fingertips as she traced the line of his shoulders out to his arms. When he turned his head toward her, she picked up her hands as if he were electric and she was afraid of the voltage.

He gazed at her, one eye open, one eyebrow raised, while the color tinted her face again and she wiped her palms on the seat of her leotard—which Simon happened to know didn't have any seat. He'd be willing to swear she'd done it unconsciously, but that hand-wiping gesture was the sexiest thing he could ever—at the moment—remember seeing. That and the fact that barely touching his shoulders made her palms sweat.

A man's ego could be spoiled rotten by that sort of thing, Simon decided. Not to mention the other parts of him. He lay still, waiting for her to put her hands on him again, slide them down to the hollow at the small of his back, and slip her fingertips under the cotton blanket draped over his lower half.

And then maybe he could turn over.

Massage was not a one-sided experience, was it?

No, definitely not, Simon decided. The voltage definitely went both ways. For some damned reason, Cleopatra O'Nile's hands on his back were the most erotic thing he'd felt since puberty. Maybe it was the reluctant, fascinated sensual awareness he could swear he felt in her fingers.

It was catching. And then, of course, he was dressed for it, being next to naked. For that matter, she was next to naked too, in that form-fitting latex number stretched a little too tightly over the curve of her hip, which was about eight inches from his nose. She curled her hands around his shoulders at the base of his neck, squeezing in just the suggestion of massage.

He found himself calculating the chances that she was after his body.

About a million to one, he acknowledged with the part of his brain that was still writing nonfiction. The entrancing Ms. O'Nile was making reckless offers she figured would never be accepted.

He ought to take her up on them just on

principle. He could count it as research: whether two adults could fit comfortably on a single massage table.

It was a definite possibility, he decided, if one of the adults happened to be on top of the other. If he turned over, for instance, and caught her wrist, brushed his thumb over her racing pulse, pressed her palm against his chest and then moved it lower . . .

She was moving it lower herself, contouring the valley of his spine with the heel of her hand while Simon's fertile imagination added a few more details of the possibilities, when the phone rang.

She froze, absolutely still except for a quick, nervous movement of her head toward the chair where his clothes, and his phones, were haphazardly draped. They spoke simultaneously. "Just ignore—" he said. "I'll get that," Cleo muttered.

She was across the room and fishing in his jacket pocket before he'd sat up on the table, and she'd picked up the phone before he'd untangled himself from the damn blanket.

"Answering for Simon Faro," she said. "No, he's not available at the moment, but if you leave your number, he'll get back to you as soon as possible."

Simon yanked the phone out of her hand, barked "Later" into the receiver, and pressed the disconnect button.

"Oh," she said faintly when he tossed one end of the blanket over his shoulder, toga-style, and tossed the phone back onto the pile of clothes on the chair. "Really, Simon, I was just . . ."

"Trying to be helpful?" he put in.

"Well . . . yes." She smiled. "Massage sessions really shouldn't be interrupted by phone calls. Don't you agree?"

"Oh, yeah."

"So I just thought I'd take a message for you. Just being . . . helpful." The dark brown eyes, soft, limpid, and, he would have sworn if he didn't know better, candid, blinked once and then held his gaze persuasively.

"Just taking a message."

"Yes, Simon," she said softly.

"And a phone number."

"In case you wanted to call back."

There was a catch in her breathing, a slight flush to her cheeks, and a faint curve to the way she held herself that spoke of physical awareness.

Damned if he didn't want to believe her. It was possible, he conceded, that she'd merely wanted to quell any distractions that would interrupt their session, and that she was a little too naive at this game to realize that you didn't take phone calls on behalf of a man whose business you didn't know.

She *was* pretty naive. Hell, she hadn't even wanted to touch him. After he'd taken off his pants, she'd procrastinated over dropping them on the chair until he'd wondered if she was about to drop the whole exercise and walk out of the room. It must have taken her three minutes to—

Light dawned as if someone had flicked the switch on a station-house lineup.

Three minutes to put his pants on the chair. Dammit, she *had* tailed him halfway across the city to get into his jeans. And he'd bet his asp she'd done it too.

"Cleo," he said, pausing to sigh expressively, "hand me my pants."

"Hand you your—"

"Yeah. From the chair there."

"But, Simon, you—"

He reached in front of her to pick them up. A quick check of the pockets was all that was needed.

"Cleo," he said reproachfully. She didn't

answer. "Did you take just a quick peek into my back pocket?"

She still didn't answer.

"And did you remove just an unimportant little computerized address book from my pants?"

She took a breath. "Simon . . . I . . . ah . . . can explain that."

"I'm sure you can. Cleo."

"I just wanted to know who . . . ah . . . I was getting involved with. You know?"

"No."

"I mean, a woman can't be too careful these days. A little research is sometimes in order."

"A little research." He knew his smile wasn't friendly and open. He watched her assess the expression. With true talent, she responded to it immediately and with faultless instinct.

"Well," she said, a hint of wronged woman straightening her spine, "it seems a little research might definitely be in order in your case. Since you have three IDs in your pocket and they're all for different identities."

"Ever hear of glass houses, Cleo?"

"And one of them," she went on, working up to outrage, "is a *police* ID."

"No, it isn't."

"Is too! Close enough anyway. You could get arrested for that! Impersonating an officer is an arrestible—"

"Impersonating a masseuse, *lady*, is even more dangerous! Especially when you're garnering phone numbers and picking pockets."

"If I didn't want to live dangerously," she shot back at him, "I wouldn't be here!"

"Where the hell would you be? And who the hell hired you to tail me instead?"

She managed to look hurt and astonished at the same time. "You think I'd do this for *money*?"

"Yeah. I do. So who was it?"

"I'm not going to—"

"Yes, you are, sweetcakes," Simon muttered, dropping his pants and bending over to snag her oversized satchel. He dragged it toward him, unzipped the opening, and started pawing through the contents.

"Wait a minute—wait just a damn minute!"

"No," he told her. His ID was in the top layer of paraphernalia. The second layer held a change of underwear and a couple of crumpled-up chocolate-bar wrappers. The middle layer held all the interesting stuff.

"You can't just—"

"Yes, I can. What's this?" Simon fished out a pair of handcuffs in what appeared to be working order, keys unattached.

"I—it's—that's part of my massage stuff."

"Handcuffs?"

"Some people have odd . . . tastes."

"I'll say. You seem to have quite a collection of IDs yourself, lady. And not one of them seems to say *Cleo*."

"Give me that!"

"Not a chance."

"Dammit!"

The door behind them opened, startling them both.

"What's going on in here?" the dragon-tattooed receptionist demanded.

Both of them spoke at once, neither comprehensible. The receptionist glanced from one to the other, stared with disapproval at the handcuffs Simon was brandishing, then crossed her arms over her chest, causing the dragon's tail to twitch. "I'm calling the cops," she announced.

The bag they'd been tugging between them dropped to the floor, landing on Simon's foot and eliciting a neat round curse.

Cleo ignored him and said, "Oh, miss . . . don't do that. I mean just—"

"I'm calling 'em!"

The woman took a heavy step toward the door, and Cleo let out a long, resigned sigh. "Why is it that calling the cops is the answer to every problem in the world?" she muttered.

Simon didn't waste time questioning an opportunity when he stumbled over one. "Don't bother," he snapped at the receptionist. "They're here."

He slapped a handcuff on Cleo's wrist, clicked the remaining one to his own, and snagged the wallet of IDs Cleo had snitched from his pocket. "Police," he barked, flashing the facsimile badge across the receptionist's line of vision. "This woman is my prisoner. We're just leaving. Thanks for your efforts at being a good citizen. I appreciate your cooperation, but you'd best leave this situation in my hands from here on."

He reached for his pants while he was talking, yanked them on under the toga, and zipped the fly with Cleo's hand resisting arrest at every move.

"Police?" the receptionist said with wariness and morbid curiosity. "What'd she do?"

Simon glanced at Cleo briefly. No telling what she was about to say; she was moving quickly past shock. Maybe she needed another jolt. "Solicitation," he said.

"*Solicitation?*" Cleo's eyebrows shot up in outrage and she yanked on his arm hard enough to pull a button off the shirt-sleeve he was trying to shove his free hand into. Simon half expected her to blurt out the truth, but she didn't break character. "When did I ever ask you for money?" she demanded.

He had to admire the question, especially under the circumstances.

"You didn't, sweetcakes. You just lifted my wallet. Now, let's go." He pulled the shirt up to one shoulder and snatched up his jacket.

"Grab your bag, Cleo," he said as he hauled her toward the door.

She had the presence of mind to obey.

THREE

Simon tossed her five-ton bag into the back of the old Jag and hustled his arrested masseuse into the driver's side ahead of him. He quickly exited the parking lot, then nearly blew the entire choreography of their escape by veering straight toward an arborvitae hedge, when Cleo yanked on his wrist.

"What the hell are you doing?" Simon spun the steering wheel and missed the hedge by inches. She yanked his wrist again, reaching for her bag in the back.

"I'm looking for the keys! And I can't . . . quite . . ."

"Dammit, Cleo, I'm trying to drive here!"

"Is that what you call it?" She pulled the bag toward her and leaned over the seat.

"Look, I'll pull over as soon as we're out of the neighborhood. Sit still."

"Forget it. I am not going to *sit still* beside a man I'm handcuffed to!"

"They're *your* handcuffs."

"What's that got to do with it?"

"Presumably you've used them before."

"Not to abduct an innocent party with a fake ID and a story that ought to make your nose grow!"

"What did you want me to do, let that desk clerk call the cops? You want to be explaining all this to Saratoga's finest?"

"Oh, hell, no. Anything but the cops."

"My feelings exactly."

She yanked on his arm. He gripped the steering wheel to keep the Jag in its own lane.

"Ah-ha!" She flipped around on the seat and pulled his wrist away from the wheel again to fiddle with the lock of the handcuffs. To his relief, the metal restraint opened and he had his hand back again.

There was a clink as his would-be masseuse dropped the handcuffs into her bag and stashed the keys in an outside zippered pocket. For a woman who was so flustered by being handcuffed to a relative stranger, he noted, she had an awful lot of facility with the equipment.

"You know what, Cleo?" he asked.

She crossed her arms in front of her spandexed chest. "I know what I'd like to know," she informed him. "I'd like to know what you think you're doing impersonating a cop and abducting a woman you never met before."

He slowed for a turn, took it, then shot her an assessing glance. "Cleo, that wasn't a real impersonation. In this neighborhood, if I wanted to impersonate a cop, I'd have my hand out."

She shut her mouth abruptly, stared at him, then frowned. Score one for Simon, he thought. Apparently he'd derailed her outrage, and he wasn't above pressing his temporary advantage. "And about the abduction part, Cleo. You know what I'd like to know?"

She held off for a minute, body language defensive and offended, arms crossed. When he didn't say anything else, she slanted him a look, chewing on her lower lip. "What?" she asked finally.

"I'd like to know what happened to that sexy little catch in your voice."

"*What* catch in my voice?"

"The one you had when you got me up on the table and told me you wanted me 'bottoms up.' "

The sudden charge of sexual awareness in the car could have been sold as a battery. They both knew what he meant.

"That was a . . . massage situation," she murmured.

"Cleo?"

"What?"

"That's a little lame, isn't it? A *massage situation?*"

"Yes."

"You followed me halfway across the city, eavesdropped on a private conversation—"

"*Private?* Well, I suppose. If you don't count the three hundred pigeons."

"They, at least, had come into the place to eat. And I think three hundred is an exaggeration."

"Two hundred ninety, then. Maybe your friend Nickel added them up on his calculator."

He glanced at her.

"What is he doing with a calculator anyway?" she asked him.

"He has a part-time job as an accountant."

"Oh, I'll just bet he does."

"Cleo," he said patiently, "give up betting. You're no good at it."

"How do you know if I'm any good at it?"

"Well, let's see." He draped a wrist over the leather-covered steering wheel. "How'd you bet in the Foreman fight?"

She gave him a long, suspicious look, then smiled, patted her hair, and murmured, "I never bet on fights, Simon. I just go to look at the half-naked bodies."

"Bodies."

"That's right."

"Two men in briefs pounding each other to a pulp, giving each other black eyes . . ."

Her smile didn't waver. "It's sooo sexy."

The buzz of the phone in his jacket pocket cut off her cat-with-the-cream smile. Her glance homed in on his phone. He could almost see her ears prick up.

He pulled the phone out of his pocket, said "Later" into it, and punched the off button with his thumb.

Cleo looked distinctly disappointed for a moment, but covered the expression quickly with a slick smile. "You know, you don't need to snub your callers on my behalf. I'll understand if you need to conduct a little phone business."

"I'm trying to give my full attention to you, Cleo."

"Oh."

"You did indicate, back at the club, that you didn't want me to be distracted by the phone."

"Well, yes, I . . ."

"After all, you've gone to a lot of trouble in search of a massage session."

She blinked once, but brazened it out. "Yes."

"Which is going to be a private matter, right? You aren't going to report back to any interested third party?"

"Certainly not!" She looked genuinely shocked.

Simon let out a resigned breath and made another turn. He wouldn't stake his life on the authenticity of her outrage, but it was pretty clear she wasn't about to tell him who her client was. He'd be willing to bet her loyalty, if not her honesty, wasn't breachable. His Cleo wasn't a come-and-go kind of woman.

So who the hell was she working for?

It had to be the bookie who'd set up shop in the middle of Ranger's sushi bar.

The operator was—so far—getting off with complete anonymity. Ranger was the one being squeezed by a local cop for "protection" money, and Ranger, with his record, wasn't in a position to squawk. Even if he handed the Saratoga Police Department a cop on the take, they'd shut him down until the case was solved. They wouldn't give a damn whether Ranger was innocent or not, and the damage to Ranger's business once they were through with their investigation probably wouldn't even prick their collective conscience. The cops would get their man, and Ranger would sink like a stone.

Simon wasn't going to let that happen. He'd backed Ranger in buying the business when the man had gotten released—and Ranger had been paying him back, both in money and in the real coin of staying straight.

That wasn't something Simon was willing to sacrifice, no matter how appealing he might find some gamin-faced babe who was out to sabotage his research. Cleo, interesting as she was, was not going to muck up his current goal.

On the other hand, losing her wasn't a good idea either. She was the only lead he had, so far, to finding the anonymous bookie. Maybe the answer to his problem was to give her what she claimed she wanted.

His butt. The idea had a certain appeal.

"Where are we going, Simon?" Jo said succinctly, ignoring his smile.

He grinned a little more. "Someplace," he said, drawing it out, "where we can have some privacy, Cleo. Someplace where we can continue with the massage," he continued. "Someplace where we won't be interrupted by inconvenient third parties."

She cleared her throat in preparation for a protest.

"How about your place?" he said.

Her place? *Her* place? Her *real* place? "Oh, no. That wouldn't work at all. My place is . . . ah . . . under repair. They're fixing the toilet," she added for verisimilitude.

"You have someone fixing your toilet while you're not there?"

"A whole crew," she said solemnly. "Probably the landlady too. And the supervisor."

"The supervisor."

"He wants to make sure the job is done right. He's a personal friend. A client, in fact," she added. The invented truths were actually spilling out of her mouth as if she'd been lying all her life. She was a little miffed, in fact, that he didn't seem to believe her.

"Quite a crowd," he said, deadpan. "I hope it's a large bathroom."

"Simon," she said reproachfully.

"Yes?"

"Distrust causes stress on the entire muscular system. You're probably getting knots in your neck."

He raised one eyebrow at her in clearly continued distrust, but she could see him shift his shoulders just slightly, as if to stretch out his neck.

She reached across the seat and put her hand on his shoulder. He glanced at the hand, and then at her face. His eyebrow rose a little more, but it wasn't distrust that he was expressing. Jo felt a tiny little rush of illicit uncoplike feminine satisfaction. She curled her fingers around the back of his neck, and a nervous thrill of sensation traveled all the way up her arm when she felt the responsive quiver of warm skin under her palm. "Why don't we go to *your* place, Simon?"

"My place." He flexed his shoulder muscles again.

"Yes."

"Cleo, Cleo," he interrupted, shaking his head, causing his hair to brush over the back of her hand in the lightest of distractions.

"What?" she said, distracted.

"I think you were right back at the Bayview. We need to get to know each other. Unresearched dates aren't a good idea these days. We need more information about each other first."

"Information?"

"Why don't we spend the weekend together, Cleo? Take our time. Not rush things. Then you wouldn't have to read my address book or pick my pockets. And I wouldn't have so many knots in my neck."

Jo removed her hand from his knots. The implication that *she* had caused his tense muscles was insulting, she told herself. And the illicit thrill tingling up her arm was going places in her body that shouldn't be involved in this assignment. "The weekend?" she said.

"Any woman who chases a man for six hours deserves more than a quick encounter, Cleo."

"You're talking about a—"

"A slow encounter," he said slowly, and

with enough implications to arouse that little thrill even when she wasn't touching him.

She licked her lips, then cleared her throat. She didn't intend to have any encounter at all with him aside from arresting him and hauling him downtown. Still, when Simon Faro murmured "Slow encounter," she felt a shiver and a funny yearning ache in the back of her throat.

As if he were reading her mind again, Simon's eyes darkened, the pupils expanding, his gaze lingering on her face while the sleek little Jag drifted toward the sidewalk at the edge of the street.

"Simon! You're going off the road!"

He glanced back at the road and casually corrected the mistake.

Her panic, Jo admitted, had been an overreaction. It wasn't like her, but the unnerving idea that Simon Faro was reading her mind was enough to send any rational undercover cop into panic, wasn't it? What if she'd been thinking about arresting him?

She hadn't, however.

She'd been thinking about sex.

She'd been thinking about sex ever since she'd met Simon Faro's gray eyes over a cup of sake an hour earlier. The idea that he was thinking about the same thing was . . .

. . . Wouldn't do. There weren't going to be any slow encounters with Simon Faro. There was going to be one quick *you're under arrest* encounter, and then she was going to be done with him, and with this case and, she fervently hoped, with undercover work entirely. She wasn't suited for it.

Or maybe she was.

"Is that your answer, Cleo?" he murmured. "You want to find out more about my driving? You want me to . . . slow down?"

The phone in Simon's back pocket buzzed. He answered it, said "Later" into the receiver before he could possibly have identified who was calling, and tucked the unit back into his pocket.

Jo glanced at the disappearing phone in frustration. Obviously, she wasn't going to get any easy information from eavesdropping on his phone calls.

She was going to have to get her information some other way.

She drew some air into her overstressed lungs, gave a toss to her teased ponytail, and met his gaze briefly one more time. "That would be a lovely idea, Simon," she said softly. "Let's get to know each other."

He glanced at her. She could almost see him processing the clues to her identity in his head, then he grinned—an expression she found worrisome—and made an illegal U-turn.

"Simon? Where are we going?"

"You ask that question a lot, Cleo."

"I like to know which way is up, Simon," she murmured.

"Don't worry, sweetcakes. You'll be a hit no matter where we go."

"Oh, but, Simon," she simpered, giving her best imitation of a sex kitten. "I'm not dressed for *just anywhere*." She batted her eyes at him. "I'm not wearing nearly enough makeup."

He glanced toward her. "Yes, you are."

"Is that supposed to be a compliment?"

"Yes," he said directly.

Jo snapped her mouth shut, nonplussed. She'd expected sarcasm, not honesty. Certainly not an actual compliment.

And he hadn't answered her question, she reminded herself, although the answer was fairly obvious. They were headed back the way they'd come, toward the Temple Bell Sushi bar, where, presumably, they'd get to know each other's preferences in raw fish, and with any luck at all, Simon Faro would do something felonious so she could arrest him. With any luck at all she could have the deed done and drive herself home to change her clothes before she showed up at the station.

Luck wasn't running her way, however. Around the corner of the park, directly in front of the Temple Bell, were two city trucks. One of them was busily attaching his rig to the front of her car.

She and Simon swore in tandem. Simon pulled the Jag into a vacant space, and they were both out of it with simultaneous slamming of the doors. She beat him to the tow-truck driver.

"Hold it right there," Jo snapped at him. He didn't even look her way as he lowered the towing rig toward her bumper.

"Listen, buddy—"

This time she rated a casual, bored glance.

What was she going to do? Tell him she was a cop? Flash her badge at him? Simon Faro was twenty feet away from her on the curb, talking to the owner of the Temple Bell, who was standing with his arms crossed and his eyes fixed on the tow trucks.

Behind him several teenagers, including the pigeon-feeding Nickel, milled around, holding pool cues.

"Who ordered these cars towed?" she demanded.

"The police, lady."

"*What* police? Who?"

"Hey," the man said, shaking his head, "Take it up with them. I'm just doin' my job here."

Out of the corner of her eye she saw Simon turn toward the restaurant, his hand going to his back pocket. He stopped, slapped his other pocket, caught sight of Jo, and strode toward her, his jaw set.

"My wallet, sweetcakes," he said.

"Oh." She dug around in her bag for about five seconds before Simon grasped her arm and ushered her into the restaurant.

"What do you think you're doing?" she demanded.

"Saving Ranger's clientele base," he shot back at her.

"How?"

"I'm paying their parking tickets up front, sweetcakes. You can thank me later. Just find me my wallet *now.*"

The Temple Bell atmosphere was confused and mildly chaotic. No one seemed to be sitting. She sideswiped a customer just inside the door with her bag before her eyes adjusted to the dim lighting, but the man didn't offer any complaints. Either he didn't care, or she'd knocked the wind out of him. Simon's guiding hand on her elbow didn't leave her time for any more than a hasty apology.

A uniformed cop was standing at the counter by the cash register, drinking a beer and watching the scene through the front window.

Rick Nielson, Jo realized with a small thrill of panic. He'd probably recognize her. She managed to turn her back before Nielson looked toward them as Simon hauled her with him across the room. She dropped her bag on a nearby chair and bent over it, giving the cop a view of her backside. She was fairly sure he wouldn't recognize her from that angle.

Why was Nielson throwing his weight around having cars towed anyway?

Out of the corner of her eye she could tell he was taking a leisurely look at her. *Ogling* was the word that came to mind.

Simon leaned over her shoulder, obstructing Nielson's line of sight, for which she was grateful, but she could have done without Simon up close and in her face. Or her ear, more precisely.

"Where the hell is it, Cleo?" he muttered. "It's a leather wallet. You've probably got it filed under stolen goods."

"No," she muttered back. "It's filed under fake IDs. Which one, by the way, are you planning to use?"

"I don't need an ID, sweetcakes. I just need cash."

She stopped rummaging to shoot him a curious look. "What for?"

"Thanks for the beer," Nielson drawled to Ranger, who'd followed them in. "You got a nice place here." He paused a moment, then said, "See you around."

Simon dug into Jo's bag.

"Wait a minute!" she bit out. "That's *my* handbag!"

"And this is my wallet." He pulled it out, opening the money compartment as he turned toward Nielson. "Officer," he said smoothly, "could I arrange to pay the parking tickets up front? And the charges for the truck, of course."

Jo shut her mouth on the outrage gathering in her chest, turned around again before Nielson got a look at her, and bent over her bag. Underwear and candy wrappers were spilling out of the top of it, while all the heavy items had sunk to the bottom, courtesy of Simon's less-than-careful sorting. She stuffed everything back in, pinched the bridge of her nose between thumb and forefinger, and chewed on the question of whether Nielson would actually take a bribe from Simon Faro, traffic violator.

It wasn't beyond the realm of possibility, though she was afraid to admit it. She was an honest cop's daughter. She'd been raised with a clear understanding of who the good guys were, and that understanding had survived her five-year career as a police officer.

She fully intended to have it survive this asinine undercover assignment too. She could only hope that in the process her quarry wouldn't get them both arrested for attempted bribery.

No mention of arrest was made, however, just the faint swish of money changing hands, and the slap of Simon's wallet as he shut it. She glanced at them and caught Nielson giving her a curious once-over. She had a feeling he wasn't going to leave until he got another look at her.

Her heart pounding, Jo put her bag over her shoulder, and stepped between Simon and Nielson, her back to the police officer.

"Darling!" she breathed, her voice husky and, she hoped, unrecognizable. She slipped her hands around Simon's neck and pulled his face down toward hers. "Thank you for saving my car! Let me make it up to you." She pulled his face close to hers and made exaggerated kissy sounds.

"Sure thing, sweetcakes," Simon murmured. She couldn't miss the irony in his tone, but he went along with the act. He wrapped a hand around her back and turned her toward the counter.

Nielson gave a cynical snicker and strolled away from them, but she couldn't see the policeman's exit.

Simon moved his hand in slow circles on her back, holding her against him in a convincing show of passion that was . . . unnerving. She couldn't seem to catch her breath, and when she took a deep gulp of air, she breathed in the scent of leather and aftershave and Simon. She could hear her own heartbeat, thrumming along under the influence of adrenaline and narrowly averted danger. *Shared* adrenaline, she realized. Shared danger. Simon's heart was beating fast too. She could feel the pulse at the side of his neck, where her fingertips pressed against his skin through the silky texture of his hair. She had the odd desire to touch the little gold stud earring, maybe with her lips. To whisper something . . .

"Simon," she whispered, making a desperate grab for her rapidly fraying self-control, "shouldn't we . . . ah . . . move now?"

"Not quite yet, sweetcakes," he murmured. Outside, a car door thunked shut, and a towing rig clanked onto the pavement as, she hoped, her car was released.

Simon let go of her, allowing her to put a few inches between their bodies. He glanced down at her bag.

"White lace panties and a nine-millimeter automatic. You're a dangerous woman, Cleo."

She willed her pulse to slow down, but it was galloping along at a pace that would have done justice to any kind of danger she could dream up. She cleared her throat, then licked her lips.

Simon's gaze hadn't left hers, and the intensity of the stare gave her the chills.

It wasn't just that he'd caught a glimpse of her white lace underwear and her gun. He'd gone along with her fake pass at him and shielded her from discovery by a cop he'd just bribed. It put her in his debt. She owed him something, and just as luck would have it, she'd suggested fairly explicitly how she could make it up to him.

Even in the relatively dim interior of the Temple Bell his gray eyes made her throat go dry. For a second, the question of just what she might do to fulfill her rash promises to Simon Faro burned through Jo's mind with an intensity that completely eclipsed the matter of how she was going to arrest him. Her gaze locked with his. He didn't move, one forearm resting casually on her shoulder, his expression riveted and a little speculative.

She wasn't sure what to make of him. What to make of them together. What to make of herself, for that matter. Her heart was still beating out a rhythm as primitive and explicit as the suggestion she'd made a moment earlier.

Maybe it was the spandex. Some unexpected side effect of her new persona. She'd succumbed to the most basic danger of undercover work. She'd gone native.

"You have a permit for that sort of thing?" Simon asked her.

She had the oddest desire to tell him the truth. To mean it. "The panties, or the gun?"

His low chuckle conveyed approval and interest, and it pleased her far more than it should have.

"You know something, Cleo? I like your style," he said softly.

What style was that? Her flustered breathlessness? Her adhesiveness? Her spandex?

Nothing, she told herself, that had anything to do with the real Mary Jo O'Neal, but there was something about being held in Simon's arms, breathing in the smell of leather and washed cotton, feeling the pressure of his hand on her back and the faint warmth of his breath on her temple, that blurred the distinctions between the real Jo and Cleo. Her answering chuckle to his compliment was low, husky, and, yes, sexy.

Simon slid his forearm down her shoulder, brushing the side of her neck with his fingertip, bringing an undeniable thrill of sensual excitement. In helping Simon Faro bribe a cop, she wasn't Jo O'Neal, dumped fiancée, dead-serious detective, YMCA-member kind of woman. The sexy glint in his gray eyes told her that, somehow, he knew that.

And Jo didn't care.

When the phone in his inside pocket

started ringing, Jo reached inside his jacket and pulled it out, then clicked it on, breathed "Later" into the receiver, and slipped it back into his pocket.

"Your phone manner's improving by leaps and bounds, Cleo," he told her.

She leaned back from the waist, batted her eyelashes at him, and responded, "I'm a fast learner."

"And a slow dancer. A good combination."

Did he think so? Did he think *they* were a good combination? Did he feel the same kind of attraction that was pulling her in, weaving a spell around her, appealing to her senses in a way that was more intoxicating than the sake served by the Temple Bell?

As if he were reading her mind, he murmured, "Cleo sweetcakes, whoever you are, you sure as hell make me want to shelve the question and just get down to simple basics."

She could feel his gaze on her face and looked up at him. Even with the touch of nothing more than a fingertip, he had her hypnotized.

She was touching him, she realized, shocked by the sudden realization. Her hands were resting on his hips, her fingertips brushing his muscular buttocks, her thumbs contouring the hard ridges of his hipbones.

He was standing with his feet slightly apart, one hand on her back, holding himself still, as if waiting for her to pull his hips toward hers and align their bodies together.

"Simon," she rasped through her tight throat, "I think I need some air."

"Good idea," he murmured. He walked her past the bar, out the door, across the street, and over a patch of newly sown grass clearly marked with Keep Off signs to the lacy, semi-secluded shade of a jogging path along which she'd tailed him a couple of hours earlier.

She was still wearing the same Reeboks, Simon noticed. She had the same trim little backside, the same stubborn commitment to her cause, but she'd added a few attractions he hadn't noticed at first chase: that little catch in her breathing, and the flush of color that didn't come from makeup. And the irresistible fact that she wanted to be kissed. Now. Here. By the man she'd been tailing for seven hours.

His Cleo was good at this game—hell, she'd faked him out twice already—but she couldn't fight her own nature.

He might as well demonstrate that fact. He turned her toward him, put his hands on her shoulders and pulled her a little closer, then lowered his mouth to hers.

She didn't resist him—not when he slanted his head to touch all the soft contours of her lips, not when he slid the tip of his tongue along the seam of her lips, not when her small, breathless gasp gave him access to the intimate inner surfaces of her mouth.

He'd promised her slow, and that was what he'd intended, but when she gave a soft moan and leaned into his body, Simon forgot slow. Instead, he gave her hot and velvet and possessive, intimate enough to make her pulse race where he laid his palm against the side of her neck and curved his thumb around her jaw, tipping her face toward his, giving his tongue the intimate rights of her mouth.

Her sleek curves were nestled against the front of his body where his jacket gaped open, her hips fitted against the juncture of his thighs, her hands soft and needful on his back, the tiny sound in the back of her throat a surrender to the heat that flared between them.

Or maybe the sounds were his. Maybe

he was the one whose hands urged her closer, locking their bodies together in a sweet, hot embrace that made the blood surge in his body and his good intentions evaporate into steam.

He spread his hand on her back, pressing her against him, shrugging open the front of his jacket with impatience born of the need to hold her.

Cleo's bag, still looped over her shoulder, slipped off, and she let it go, uncaring.

It landed on his foot.

The thud, the clink, and the sudden pain in his toes broke through the haze of sensuality. They separated; Cleo said, "Oh" in a dismayed tone, and Simon gritted his teeth and grimaced.

She stared at him, her eyes wide, the pupils still dilated with desire, then she started to laugh, the sound husky and breathless and sexy as hell.

Simon grinned reluctantly, then tipped his head back and let his shoulders relax, his hands still around her back, his body still straining for the continuation of what he'd started.

It would have to wait, of course. He wasn't going to take things any further in a public park in broad daylight, no matter how good she felt. Or how little she was wearing.

Or who she was.

He eased his foot out from under the bag, hearing the clink of her handcuffs and the rustle of her crumpled chocolate-bar wrappers.

And her nine-millimeter automatic. Simon stared at her as a piece of truth snapped into place, giving him a sudden, blindsiding insight.

Her nine-millimeter, *police-issue* automatic.

The clutch in his stomach was a combination of shock, confusion, and sheer awe.

He'd just had his socks kissed off by a Saratoga cop.

FOUR

"Simon? Where are we going?"

Simon glanced across the seat at her, then flicked his gaze back to the road. *That was one hell of a question.*

Technically, they were going north on the expressway, three cars behind the red Infiniti occupied by Nickel and the group of teenage kids he'd left the Temple Bell with.

Nontechnically, they were lurching down the center lane of one of life's crash tests. He was the test dummy and Cleo was the sand in the gas tank.

A cop.

That must have been why she didn't want to be seen by Nielson. It also explained the persistence, the chutzpah, and the handcuffs.

He should have known. He'd been faked out before, but not this monumentally. How the hell had he let himself fall for it?

"Simon?" she said again.

He felt a reaction to that husky voice travel along his upper arms and angle down his chest and stomach, lighting up all the masculine nerve endings along the way with the remembered imprint of her body against his.

She was a *cop*, Simon reminded himself. He was in a car entertaining carnal thoughts about a cop who'd claimed she liked watching half-naked men being beaten up, and carried handcuffs in her bag. Maybe, Simon thought grimly, this last period of abstinence had been a little too long.

"We're following the red Infiniti two cars ahead of us," he said.

"I know that much. I was asking if you have any idea where we're going."

"Not a clue, sweetcakes."

Her eyebrows rose, and Simon braced himself for further comment, but apparently she thought better of it, shut her mouth, and said nothing.

Which was just as well. He didn't need a lengthy conversation with a cop in spandex who could raise his temperature a few notches every time he thought about her whispering in his ear with that sexy voice. Especially since her first words were likely to be "You're under arrest."

This was not a good time for Simon to get arrested. Not before he nailed Ranger's bookie and secured his ex-cellmate's future as an honest businessman. Since Ranger had gotten out, he'd been clean enough to eat off of, but the situation with Nielson had been close. Ranger had knuckled under the pressure and wanted to pay him off. Simon had spent the better part of an all-nighter arguing Ranger out of it. Once Ranger paid, there'd be no honest way out; he'd be guilty by implication. Simon had managed to convince him that getting the goods on Nielson—names, dates and figures—and threatening to go public was the only leverage they had.

Unfortunately he hadn't had a chance so far to make much progress. He'd still been in shock, not to mention an astonishing level of arousal, when Nickel had pulled a quick and suspiciously smooth exit from Ranger's place with a small group of teenagers who looked like they should be wearing tennis whites and prep-school ties. Simon wasn't absolutely sure what Nickel had in common with a bunch of private-school yuppies, but it sure as hell wasn't their yacht-club memberships.

Maybe hustling Cleo into his car to follow them hadn't been the most prudent move, but, truth to tell, prudent didn't seem to be his style lately. And he hadn't had any good options. He couldn't leave her back at Temple Bell, where she might arrest someone else. And instinct had told him that if he wanted to find out what Nickel was up to, he'd better do it soon. Ex-cons like Ranger, whose restaurants were being used for illegal betting, didn't have a long shelf life. Neither did unauthorized investigators being tailed by undercover cops who wanted to arrest them. The million-dollar question was what to do with her now.

The Infiniti made an abrupt lane change, and Simon followed suit, eliciting an alarmed little squeak from Cleo as she was thrown against him. She covered it with a polite laugh, pushed herself upright, and immediately removed her hand from his thigh.

Simon gritted his teeth again. No, he decided, the *real* million-dollar question was what she'd been doing kissing him back.

He followed the Infiniti down the exit

ramp and glanced toward her. She was scrunched against the door as far away from him as possible, one leg curled under her backside, one hand firmly gripping the armrest. Her posture indicated she'd rather throw herself out of the moving vehicle than risk touching him again. He found the attitude, perversely, sexy as hell. Ms. O'Nile, despite the Cleopatra act, had lost it when she kissed him. He would have sworn to it. The way her pulse had raced was real. And the way she'd curved that sweet, slim body against him hadn't been calculated.

And that sound she made in the back of her throat . . .

She shot him a quick furtive glance, as if she sensed him covertly studying her.

Simon snapped his gaze back to the road and clenched his jaw a little harder.

All right, so now he knew she was a cop. It didn't seem to make any difference in his attraction to her.

Nickel's cronies turned, drove too fast along a tree-shaded street, and took the main gate onto the campus of a small private school with a good reputation and a large budget. Simon followed discreetly and parked behind one of the academic buildings when the Infiniti pulled into a parking space behind the dorms. Nickel didn't even give a glance toward Simon's car when he followed the kids in. Careless of him not to notice he'd been followed, Simon thought, but then, he was probably blinded by the glow of potential profits.

Cleo was looking around at the campus with interest. "Nickel has friends at St. Mark's?"

"Oh, yeah," Simon said. "Nickel speaks a universal language."

"Latin or mathematics?" she asked sweetly.

Simon gave her a quick enigmatic grin. "Wait here, Cleo."

She didn't say yes.

"Look," he improvised, "keep an eye on the door, would you? If the kids come out, cut them off at the pass."

"And how am I supposed to do that? I'm a masseuse, Simon, not a . . ."

She must have seen something in his face that killed the remaining line of fabrication. Her voice trailed off, and she watched him warily. "Just open the car door and give 'em a glimpse of spandex, Cleo," he said. "That ought to do it."

He got out of the car, slammed the

door, and let out a long breath before he headed toward the dorm.

Jo watched him go, then let out a long breath of her own and settled back against the seat.

Simon's long strides covered the back lawn of the dorm, and his shoulders flexed inside the jacket as he hauled the door open. He didn't give her so much as a single glance.

Jo chewed her lip, telling herself what she felt was the familiar frustration of unanswered questions. She had to admit to an element of resentment at being left sitting in the car. She *hated* being ditched.

She especially hated being ditched, doubted, and teased by a man wearing an earring and three cellular phones.

As soon as the door swung shut behind Simon, Jo fished her own phone out of her bag and punched in the chief's number. It was probably a mistake, she decided, listening to the ring. She hadn't yet arrested her subject, she didn't, at the moment, know what he was doing, and she didn't have a clue what was going on, but any distraction—even a conversation with her boss— was preferable to sitting on her ill-clad tush and thinking about the errors in judgment she'd already made. The list was notable: she'd lost him twice, been cuffed and abducted, and a known felon had gotten his hands on her gun.

There was also the matter of where else he'd had his hands, but Jo was working hard at ignoring that particular lapse of judgment.

"Randall," the voice on the phone said.

"Jo O'Neal," she responded. For some reason the name didn't sound quite right. She'd been on this job too long, she decided.

"O'Neal," the chief said, his voice brightening. She could hear him sitting up straighter and setting down his coffee cup. "You on your way in? You need backup? What?"

Jo pulled the phone away from her ear and frowned at it. She'd known her boss was overeager on this case, but backup? What'd he have in mind? The marines? "No," Jo said. "I don't need backup. What I need is some answers to a couple of questions."

"Like what?" the chief said. He didn't sound nearly as happy as he had seconds before.

"Like, what if this guy isn't making book?"

For a span of sharp silence there was no reply, then the chief said with an edge to his voice, "Then you find out what he is doing. And you bring him in for it."

"I don't think you want me to bring him in for what he's done so far, Chief."

"Why not?"

"Because it involved bribing a cop."

There was another silence, this one blue with unspoken language. "What'd he do?" the chief said finally. "Fix a ticket?"

"Something like that. But not exactly."

"Not exactly?"

"Chief, I think we need to discuss this. In person. Not over the phone."

"Listen to me, O'Neal. You just do your job. You bring this guy in. We'll philosophize about it later."

Philosophize about it later? What did that mean? Bribery was a philosophical question? Or maybe that the chief knew about Nielson and wanted to ignore it? Wanted her to ignore it? "Just trying to figure out exactly what my job is, Chief," she said with her own edge.

"If you're having doubts about it, O'Neal, let me make it clear. This guy's a bookie. You're a cop. You need any help interpreting that?"

If she did, Jo decided, the chief clearly didn't want to hear about it.

She took a deep breath. "This sushi bar where Faro hangs out—the one that's owned by his ex-cellmate. The guy has a teenager working there."

Over the line there was a slurp of coffee. "The owner's nephew. The kid's a chip off the old block. Been arrested a couple of times. But he had a smart lawyer."

"Let me guess. Faro got him the lawyer."

"That's right. The kid's probably working for him. Some kind of bookie-in-training."

Jo digested that. "Why isn't he working for Ranger?"

"I don't know. Maybe Ranger's too busy leadin' the life of a saint. Turns out this two-bit bookie's got character, if you read the book Faro wrote in the joint. Ranger came out of that one a damn *hero*. Guess who the bad guys were?"

"I haven't read it," Jo said.

"Yeah, well—don't."

"Did Ranger get anything out of this literary project?"

"Yeah. Faro set him up in the sushi business when he got out."

"Set him up?" Jo said, surprised. She frowned, staring across the lawn at the door where Simon had disappeared. "He has that kind of money?"

"Yeah," her boss said shortly.

"And he was sent up for *stealing cars*?"

There was a pause. "One car," the chief said. "A 'sixty-five Thunderbird. It happened to belong to the county commissioner."

"How unfortunate," Jo murmured blandly.

"No law says criminals can't be stupid," her boss suggested.

And no law said cops had to be.

"Correct me if I'm wrong, Chief," she said carefully, "but I'm getting the offbeat idea that Simon Faro might be following a pattern here. Maybe making book isn't his main line of work these days. Maybe writing books and articles is. Maybe he's writing about something the department doesn't want him to write about."

She sensed a rise in blood pressure. "Listen, O'Neal. You're not out there to get offbeat ideas. You're out there to do your job. If there's any other job to be done, you let the appropriate branch of the department do it."

"Okay, Chief, but the question is—"

"The question is, O'Neal, what the hell do you think you're talking about? Are you on the team or not?"

Her boss's question cut to the basics, all right, Jo acknowledged. She was a detective. Her loyalty was to the department. Crooked cops were the business of Internal Investigations, which probably wouldn't welcome half-bottomed advice from a rookie detective on her first undercover assignment.

Her business was apprehending crooks from the general population. And Simon Faro, no matter what his other line of work, probably qualified. She knew the procedure: Get some hard evidence, arrest him, bring him in, let the courts sort out the rest.

"I'm on the team, Chief," she said.

"Don't forget it, O'Neal."

Simple, straightforward, no second thoughts required. So why was she having them?

"I won't, Chief. But—"

He hung up in her ear.

Jo grimaced at the phone, then clicked it off and tossed it into her bag. Her boss could use some help with his phone manners. Hadn't he ever heard the word *goodbye?*

Probably not, she decided, sighing. The chief's patience was inversely proportional to his blood pressure, which she'd guess was currently somewhere in the red zone.

She doubted it would go down for anything short of her delivering Simon Faro, on a platter, handcuffed and flambéed.

Which was exactly what she was going to do, Jo told herself. It was her job. She was a cop. One of the bad guys, in Simon Faro's view of the world.

On the other team.

And she'd always been a team player. That was the problem with Simon Faro, she acknowledged, chewing her lip and unconsciously playing with the neck of her T-shirt. The excitement. The challenge. The secret, illicit thrill of . . . of undercover work. That had to be the complication that was upsetting all her cherished notions of herself. She'd never been tempted by forbidden fruit before. Or any fruit, for that matter. Not like this. Not until Simon.

Not until *Faro*, she amended. The man she was going to arrest. She had no doubt he would bend the law to suit his own purposes, all in the name of research. And she didn't have any compunctions about busting him for it.

In spite of the way he kissed.

She did not, she told herself, yanking open the car door, feel like one of the bad guys. And she was not going to let Simon Faro confuse her purpose, no matter where he'd had his hands.

She slammed the door on the old Jag unnecessarily hard, but the noise went unnoticed on the quiet campus.

There was no sign of Simon, but Jo noticed a kid with a partially shaved head climbing down the drainpipe from an open window on the third floor of the next building over.

She had to admit the kid had style. Nickel was negotiating the drainpipe as if he'd spent half his life sneaking out of his girlfriends' upper-story windows. He was two-thirds of the way down before he caught sight of Jo heading toward him.

Nickel didn't waste time on surprise reactions. With judgment she suspected had been honed by practice, he made a spectacular leap, landed like a cat, and took off. Jo sprinted after him.

He was fast, but so was Jo. She stayed ten feet behind him across two lawns and a sidewalk, and when Nickel slowed to leap over a wrought-iron fence, Jo launched herself at him, sending them both hurtling over the railing.

On his back, with the wind knocked out of him, Nickel mouthed a word that was either extremely profane or highly imaginative, but his expression was more resigned than angry. He let his head drop back on the lawn, gave up the struggle, and concentrated on breathing with Jo sitting on his chest.

"Jeez," he muttered finally. "No wonder you caught him." Nickel wheezed, coughed once, then raised his head to look at her. His gaze strayed down her spandex-clad body, and his expression grew a little confused. The combination of surprise and disbelief would have been comical if it weren't just a wee bit insulting.

Underneath his street-grunge style, the young hoodlum had smooth skin, straight teeth, and a boyish, take-me-home glint in his eye that probably made teenage hearts throb. He and Simon no doubt shared the same problem with those pesky, admiring females. Maybe she should have landed on him harder.

"So what were you doing in that dorm, Nickel?"

He raised his head again, his eyes lit with the hope of an easy escape from a difficult question. "I was just"—he wheezed—"seein' a friend. But they weren't—home."

"So you climbed down the drainpipe?"

"Yeah. I just . . ."

"What's wrong with the door, Nickel? When someone's not home, you usually just walk out the door."

"Oh, man—" Nickel raised his head again. "You think you could get off me? I'm not goin' anywhere."

Jo assessed him for a minute, then shifted her weight off Nickel's chest and let him sit up. A rumpled fifty-dollar bill fell out of his pocket onto the lawn.

He shot Jo a guilty glance as he stuffed it back in.

"Change for a fifty, Nickel?"

"My friend loaned me some money."

"Uh-huh."

"Really, just a—"

"Fast fifty?"

"Yeah."

"And a quick exit down the drainpipe?"

"I didn't steal it, if that's what you mean.

You can ask the kid that gave it to me. His name's Jacobson. And really, he's—"

"What's Simon got to do with this, Nickel?"

"Simon?" His voice rose in surprise.

"Yeah. *Simon,*" Jo said. "Why the drainpipe routine? You knew he went in there after you."

"No," the teenager said, shaking his head vehemently. "Nothin' to do with Simon. Nothing. Absolutely nothing."

"Well," Jo said, watching him. "I guess we'll find out soon, huh?"

Pure teenage panic flashed into Nickel's eyes. "Listen, you're not gonna tell him you saw me, are you? No, you can't do that, lady. Simon'll kill me. I mean, really. That's why I had to climb out the window. You don't want to see it, lady, if Simon catches me."

He'd started edging away from her, but Jo judged he was still too short of breath to outdistance her if he tried to run. She crossed her arms over her chest. "What I ought to do is call the police, Nickel."

He closed his eyes in defeat. "Yeah. Okay. You got a car? Maybe we could go right now, before Simon—"

"Try again, Nickel," she snapped. "You

don't think I'm going to believe you're about to turn yourself in to the nearest police station. Now, what's the deal with *Simon*?"

The teenager sighed, looked defeated, and then shrugged. "Oh, man. He's gonna be"—the kid sighed again—"real ticked off."

Which didn't answer the question, Jo noted, but she thought she had her answer anyway. Nickel's youthful panic was a pretty classic case of I'm-going-to-be-grounded-for-life teenage woes. It seemed his relationship with Simon was more parental than criminal. She sighed herself, echoing Nickel. "I have a feeling he's already real ticked off, kid."

"Oh, man." Nickel dropped his head back on the grass and stared up at the sky. "I shoulda stayed in bed this morning." He assessed Jo unhappily, then, with a glimmer of desperate optimism, said, "Maybe you could, you know, put in a good word for me? You know, when Simon's in a better mood?"

"Me?" Jo squeaked.

"Yeah. I mean, you know, at the right moment. When he might be more . . .

you know . . . relaxed. Like . . . you know . . ."

Unfortunately, she did. "You were right the first time, Nickel," she muttered. "You should have stayed in bed this morning."

"Hey—no offense. I mean, I didn't even know Simon *had* a girlfriend. Well—" he qualified, "I saw you in the park, but I didn't know you were *traveling* together."

Saw them in the park? The muscle at the side of Jo's face twitched. She felt an unmistakable flush creeping up her face.

Nickel frowned at her, beginning to get a clue that the conversation had somehow gone awry. "Hey—man—I think it's great that Simon has a woman, you know? He really needs that. You know, I don't mean just the stuff in the park, but someone he can really—you know—trust."

Someone he could trust.

The involuntary sound that escaped from her throat was *not*, she told herself, a niggling spurt of guilt.

Nor was it a reaction to the thought of herself as Simon Faro's woman.

Before she could speak, Nickel looked over her shoulder, and muttered a heartfelt obscenity. Jo glanced back to see Simon bearing down on them across the lawn at a dead run. The expression on his face sent a tingle of apprehension up her spine. She was a trained cop. She could handle Simon Faro, she thought as she hastily got to her feet, wiping her palms on the seat of her leotard.

Before she knew it, Nickel had scrambled to his feet, tripped once, and taken off in the opposite direction from Simon.

"Hey!" she called out. Professional instinct kicked in, and she made a sprinter's start after him.

"Hold it, sweetcakes," Simon shouted from behind her. His fingers closed on the back of her leotard and held on. Jo yelped as she snapped back against his chest, taking him down hard.

It was the second time in five minutes she'd landed on a male. Simon, she couldn't help noticing, was a lot harder, a lot bigger, and a lot more . . . something.

She craned her neck around to glare at him as she tried to get off his chest. Simon pulled her down on top of him again, her elbows in his chest, and held her by the upper arms in a firm grip.

"Let go of me!"

"No."

"Your teenage hoodlum is getting away! Let me up!"

"Forget it, sweetcakes. I'm not turning you loose on Nickel."

She pushed against him. "Why *not*?"

"Because Nickel has enough troubles already."

A flush of outrage shot adrenaline through her muscles, but it was no match for Simon's strength and determination. "What does that mean?" she demanded. "*I'm* supposed to be the trouble?"

Jo realized she was losing control of this situation. In a desperate move she tried to bring her knee up. A split second later she was on her back with Simon on top of her, his hands pinning her wrists to the ground beside her head.

Jo's anxiety blossomed into full-blown panic.

The look on his face as he loomed over her, his eyes blazing, the cords at the side of his neck taut, made her mouth go dry. He did something to her that she didn't understand. Something dangerous. "You're making a big mistake, Simon!" she threatened, but the words came out in a husky quiver that wouldn't have scared a schoolboy.

They certainly didn't convince Simon.

In fact, he seemed to take them as some kind of challenge. The position they were in suggested something highly explicit, and his mouth curved upward at the corners with a touch of pure male sensuality. She wasn't highly experienced at detecting the signs of masculine sexual interest, but since she'd met Simon she seemed to have developed a whole barrage of newly activated feminine receptors.

"A big mistake," he repeated thoughtfully. "The thing is, sweetcakes, you seem to be making it too."

"What are you . . . talking about?"

"That. Right there. That little catch in your voice." He loosened his grip, and his thumbs lightly caressed the sensitive skin at her pulse points.

"That's because you're—on top of me," she said breathlessly.

"It's about time," he muttered, bringing his face a little closer to hers.

"No!" she blurted out, her voice high. "Absolutely not! I'm not going to—"

He stared at her in fascination, his gaze focused on her mouth. "You're not going to what?" he murmured. "Kiss me? Too late for resolutions, Cleo. You already have." His mouth curled smugly. "Maybe we could give it another try though. After all, we were just getting started when you . . . ah . . . dropped your gun on my foot." He brushed the back of one knuckle down the side of her face, and illicit responses shimmered along the surface of her skin to all the feminine centers of her body.

He drew his hand along the loose neckline of her T-shirt, dipping toward her breasts. Jo opened her mouth to protest. What came out was a soft whimper. Simon's eyes darkened, the pupils dilated with intentions she understood only too well.

"We're not starting anything, Simon," she said breathlessly, her heart pounding.

"Tell you what, Cleo," he murmured as the back of his fingers brushed over the top of her breast, "if you don't like it, you can call the police."

Panic exploded inside her, chased by hot rivulets of desire. What had he meant by that remark? Did he know she was a cop?

The back of his knuckles circled the edge of her breast, tempting and teasing, distracting her completely, making her wonder where he'd touch her next. The heat of his gaze burned through her, calling up enough answering heat to melt bones. Just the thought of him kissing her again made her dizzy. Any moment now, she thought giddily, the earth was going to start moving. Maybe it was a good thing she was lying down.

"What do you say, Cleo?" Simon murmured, leaning close. His breath stirred the damp tendrils at the edge of her hair line. The heat of his palm warmed the outside of her breast and the touch of his thumb brushed the inner slope. "Do you like this?"

She murmured something indecipherable, but they both knew it wasn't *no*. Shivers of anticipation were racing along her nerve endings and strumming on her vocal cords. She should be stopping him, but she was doing no such thing. What was the matter with her?

"Simon," she sighed. "Come here."

He'd let go of her hands, she realized, dazed. And she was cupping the back of his thighs, molding the taut muscles with her palms, brushing over his hips and his back, sliding her fingers around the back of his neck to pull him closer.

"Anywhere you want, sweetcakes. Just say the word."

At the touch of his mouth she felt a pulse of pleasure that made her gasp. Simon made his own sound, half moan, half growl, and slanted his mouth over hers, his control suddenly released. The kiss was hot, hungry, and raw.

"Excuse me?"

The voice from the other side of the hedge didn't register for a few seconds on what was left of Jo's consciousness, but Simon went still. Momentarily he removed his lips from hers, sighed deeply, then sat back on his haunches and turned toward the hedge.

The man who was staring at them over the bushes blushed deeply and ran a hand through longish gray hair, then pushed his glasses higher onto his nose. "I thought you were a couple of students," he said primly.

Simon grinned, sighed again, and said, "No. We're faculty."

FIVE

She was taking her clothes off.

Simon clutched the steering wheel and carefully eased off on the gas pedal. He'd helped her up from the lawn and walked her back to the car, hoping that the anatomical signs that their encounter had been more than platonic weren't too obvious. His body was reluctantly just getting the message that all that testosterone wasn't going to be needed after all.

Now she was taking her clothes off. "Cleo," he said with careful courtesy, "what are you doing?"

She'd peeled herself out of the leotard and stuffed it into her bag, which she was now rummaging through. Without the aid of the leotard to keep the T-shirt in place, the stretched-out neck had slipped halfway down to her elbow—a tantalizing prospect, since he knew for sure she wasn't wearing underwear. She pulled out the padded jacket she'd had on earlier, jammed her hands into the sleeves, and, despite the fact that the afternoon had warmed to seventy-five degrees, zipped it up to her neck. She rummaged again, came up with her pants, and started pulling them on over the tights, shoes and all.

"Planning for an early winter?" he asked.

"No," she said curtly, then muttered, "unfortunately."

Simon shut his mouth on the next question. He hadn't needed to ask the first one, really. Five minutes earlier she'd been writhing on the grass and whispering his name in a come-hither voice. Now she was cocooning herself in layers of padding sufficient for any unexpected game of strip poker. They both knew why.

"Cleo," he said, giving her a glance, "isn't that a little like locking the barn door after the cows are out?"

"The cows," she said firmly, "are back in." She locked the zipper tab up under her chin.

"I'm doing sixty-five on this freeway, Cleo. I don't think you have to worry about the cows."

She gave him a reproachful look—wide brown eyes, faintly trembling lower lip. "You're the one who told me I had grass stains on the seat of my tights."

Simon felt the first twinge of his conscience. He made a point of tuning it out. "I just wanted you to get in the car, Cleo."

"Why?" she demanded.

"So we could stay with Nickel, before he falls in the Sarlac Pit and gets his toenails chewed off."

When she didn't answer, Simon glanced at her and caught the faintly troubled frown on her face. Then she said, "Oh."

Simon frowned back at her.

"Do you do this often?" she said finally. "Keep Nickel's toenails from getting chewed off?"

It wasn't what he'd expected her to ask. Not a Cleo question. Not a cop question either. Her fingers were still glued to the zipper tab she'd pulled up under her chin, the brown eyes serious under the stray tendrils of dark hair that had escaped from the ridiculous hairdo. She wanted to know, he realized. It was an honest question.

"He's basically a good kid," Simon said. "Just a little too bright for his own good. He'll turn out fine if he manages to stay out of trouble for the next couple of years. And if he stays out of the clutches of the Youth Services Department."

"The bad guys," she murmured.

Simon didn't answer.

"That's going to take some doing."

"Yeah. Whatever it takes."

"Nickel's making book, isn't he? That's what he was doing at St. Mark's. That's why he had fifty-dollar bills falling out of his pocket."

Simon gave her an oblique look. It would be safest to tell her nothing, but she seemed to figure things out on her own anyway.

"Yeah, he probably is," he said finally.

"Does that have anything to do with why all the cars in front of the Temple Bell were being towed?"

"I think so. That's what I'm trying to find out."

"That—" She hesitated, then said, "That cop was shaking down Ranger, wasn't he?"

Her casual tone of voice didn't disguise the edge of revulsion in the words *shaking down*. Ms. O'Nile, Simon reflected, was not okay with the idea of her crooked crony. The thought was interesting. It almost, in fact, put them on the same side.

Except for the small matter of Cleo wanting to arrest him and throw him in jail.

"Simon?" she said. That soft, slightly breathless hitch was back in her voice, hesitant, unconscious, a little vulnerable. Simon's conscience made another series of inappropriate noises at him. He hung up on it.

"As it turned out, Cleo, *I* was the one who got shaken down, rescuing your car."

"Yes, I suppose that's technically true," she said a little primly.

"It's literally true too, Cleo."

"Would you . . . ah . . . like me to reimburse you?"

Reimburse him? What was she planning to do—submit it on her expense account under bribery reimbursements? Simon shot her a disbelieving look. She gazed back at him, her expression wary.

Insight dawned. His Cleo was trying to convince herself that she hadn't really lost control back there on the lawn behind the hedges.

For some reason it irritated him.

"You're a little late, Cleo," he drawled. "The occasion for reimbursement would have been back at the Temple Bell, right after you returned my wallet. I think we should just stick with the physical stuff."

"The . . . physical stuff?" she said, as if the idea were completely foreign to her.

Simon nodded. "Massage table, bottoms up, pants off? Any of that ring a bell? Cleo?"

"I . . . thought we were going to get to know each other first, Simon, weren't we?"

"We've made a start on that, Cleo, don't you think?"

"Oh, I don't know. I mean, we haven't really—it takes time to establish—"

"Sweetcakes, we were communicating like a house on fire back there on the lawn."

"That was—it wasn't—I was just—"

"Just what?"

"Just—"

"Cleo," he said patiently, "you're either blushing, or you have that jacket zipped up too tightly."

"I am *not* blushing."

"Face it, Cleo. The cows have already been out. And what's more, they were having a hell of a good time."

"I'll let you know when my cows are

having a good time, thank you! And it will not be in the grass behind the hedges with faculty members looking on!"

The no-nonsense, take-no-prisoners tone was back in her voice. Simon felt his spirits lifting already. "We could have picked a better place," he agreed mildly and drove on.

"Simon? Where are we going?"

"We're going to see a man about a horse, Cleo. Several men, in fact. You have any hunches you want to play?"

"You mean—horse racing?"

"Yeah. Ever heard of it?"

"Of course I've heard of it. The track is back that way, Simon."

"I know. We're not going to the track."

"Oh. We're talking about off-track betting?"

He smiled at her.

"You're trying to find out who Nickel was working with, aren't you?" she asked.

"If he *was* working with someone."

"Oh. How are you going to do that, Simon?"

"I'm glad you asked that," he told her. "Because we do have to discuss tactics if we're going to work on this together. Chasing down potential bookies and knocking the holy sawdust out of them is a method that lacks . . . ah . . . subtlety. You'll need to refine your approach a little bit."

"*Refine* my approach?"

"Of course," he said blandly, "if you don't think you can manage that, I could always just dump you off at the Temple Bell, where I found you, and . . ."

Her jaw was clenched too tightly for speech, he imagined, but she finally unzipped her jacket.

"I'll handle the approach, *sweetcakes*," she said finally. "You just get us to the bookies."

Simon tried to hide his smile. "There's a clean white shirt in the bag in the back," he said, "if you want to cover up your grass stains."

Simon grabbed one final glance at the grass stains as she bent over the seat for the shirt.

His Cleo was back.

God help him.

The bar where they started their research was crowded, lively, and in violation of several codes. The games in the back room were in full illegal swing. Misdemeanors were probably being committed by everyone in the place except Simon.

Their plan was simple: They would approach one or two well-connected bookies and see what Simon could learn. Cleo's role was to act ditzy, make a few ill-informed bets, and lose enough of Simon's money to put everyone in a talkative mood. He guided her to an empty barstool and nodded subtly toward the man seated next to her, a short Danny DeVito look-alike.

"Simon darling, I could use just a wee bit more money."

He shot her a skeptical look, but reached for his wallet.

"You're an expensive date, Cleo."

She smiled at him, batting her eyelashes. "You get what you pay for, Simon."

He pressed a twenty into her palm. "Not yet, I haven't."

Jo chewed her lower lip, absently slipping the twenty into the back pocket of her jeans. She'd gone for the desert-island look, making her jeans into shorts and knotting Simon's shirt at the waist. Her new makeshift outfit seemed to work even better at establishing her identity as a sexpot. She'd fielded all innuendoes with a Cleo-like wave of her hand and a suggestive smile, but her latest transformation seemed to be working on Simon too. She could feel the heat of his eyes on her.

Jo chewed on her lip again. For some reason he elicited some latent female response she hadn't thought herself capable of. In fact, he seemed to have a habit of getting unexpected reactions from her. Goading her, teasing her, pushing all her buttons.

She glanced at him without really meaning to, and found him looking back at her. Her heart did a mildly panicked skip at the intensity of his gaze, and she quickly looked away.

She had to concentrate on the job at hand. If she could find out who had hired Nickel, she could arrest whoever was guilty, serve him up to the chief in place of Simon Faro, and wrap up her undercover career once and for all, before it got . . . complicated.

She turned her attention to the television over the bar that was tuned to coverage of the horse races. It was time to make an ill-informed bet, but Jo was unsure how to proceed.

None of the usual conversational openings seemed appropriate, so she smiled at the man next to her, leaned against the bar, and murmured, "Venetian Red, to win, in the sixth."

The bookie squinted at her with one eye closed and said, "You're kidding. *Venetian Red?* What's that—the color of your toenail polish?"

"Red's always been my color," Jo confided. "And Simon said I could pick any horse I wanted. Didn't you, Simon darling?"

"Oh, I bet he did," the bookie commented, giving Jo a quick leer.

"Do you know Simon?" she asked innocently.

"Yeah. I know Simon." The two men nodded at each other.

"I'm Cleo. I'm Simon's personal masseuse."

"Masseuse." The bookie raised an eyebrow. "Good for Simon."

"We were"—Jo waved a hand airily—"drawn to each other. Sometimes you just get lucky, you know?"

"I bet he did," the bookie said.

Jo was counting on the fact that he'd bet on almost anything. Now, if he'd just get on with doing it, she could get on with her plan. "Luck has just been with me lately," she improvised. Simon was rubbing the center of his forehead with two fingers. "And I owe so much of it to Simon," she said.

"Mmm. You stick with Venetian Red in the sixth and you'll owe him more."

Jo ignored the gambling advice and went on. "Simon rescued my car from some nasty old policeman who was having it towed. Why, if it weren't for Simon, I'd be walking the streets."

"Was that in front of Ranger's place? This morning?" the man asked.

"Yeah," Simon said finally, sounding reluctant. "The cops seemed to think there was some action at Ranger's place, and wanted to be cut in."

"Right." The man shrugged. "Cost of doin' business."

"Ranger's not doing business," Simon said.

"No?" The man glanced at Jo again, apparently decided she was harmless. "So who is?" he asked Simon.

"Nobody, now. But Ranger's young nephew had designs on the territory."

"Oh, yeah?" The man grinned and shook his head indulgently. "Chip off the ol' block, huh? Smart kid. Entrepreneurial spirit."

He wasn't joking, Jo realized. The man

thought Nickel's fledgling gambling career was admirable.

"He's not working for you, then?" Simon asked.

"Me? Naw. But if he ever . . . you know . . ."

Jo crossed her arms in front of her and covertly flexed her fingers, anticipating the feel of her detective's shield. With a little luck she could get him booked and delivered before eight.

"Hey, lookit that," the bookie said. "They're talkin' about the sixth."

"Oh, Simon," Jo breathed. "Look. They're talking about the sixth. And I don't have any money down."

Simon's look passed from dubious to suspicious.

"Oh, and Venetian Red will be running." She leaned over the bar, just a trifle closer to the bookie beside her. "And I have *such* a hunch," she purred at him, then batted her eyelashes a couple of times for good measure.

"Well, Cleo honey, if you really have a hunch . . ."

"Cleo," Simon interrupted. "Let's dance."

She frowned at him. "Let's what?"

"Come on, sweetcakes." Simon caught her by the wrist and pulled her away from the bar, then clamped her into a body lock and waltzed her across the floor toward the jukebox.

"What are you doing?" Jo demanded.

"Protecting my sources, sweetcakes."

"Protecting your—" She sputtered to silence.

"That's right, Cleo. Just in case you were sustaining some stray inclination to call the cops."

"Call the cops?" she repeated. She was beginning to sound like a broken record, but the combination of surprise at Simon's interruption and the effect of his determined, well-muscled body against hers was having its effect on her thought processes.

"Forget it, Cleo."

She eased as far away from him as she could, and murmured, "Oh, but, Simon, even if I did have just a tiny, wee notion about calling the cops, it was only because that man was obviously engaged in illegal activities. Wasn't he?"

"Not yet," Simon said.

"But any moment—"

"Cleo," he said curtly, "forget it. No one is getting arrested tonight."

"No one is getting . . ."

"That's right. Arrested. No one. Not tonight."

When she didn't answer him, he gave her a long, probing look, as if he were trying to read her. "I'm trying to keep Nickel out of this, Cleo," he said finally, "and I just need a little time."

It wasn't what she'd expected to hear. Startled, she felt her throat close around a wordless response.

His hand, holding hers as they danced, squeezed her fingers, the increased pressure just barely noticeable, perhaps unconscious. "Okay, Cleo?"

Something in the sound of his voice changed the rhythm of her pulse. He'd demanded, he'd finessed, he'd ignored, but he'd never *asked*.

She stared back at him and read a flicker of something else beneath his determination. Vulnerability. Concern—for Nickel, maybe, or possibly Ranger. Either way, it was an acknowledgment that she could hurt him.

Jo felt her heart lurch. She'd thought he was a hard-hearted cynic. The depth of emotion she saw in the harsh lines of his face now caught her completely off guard.

She was a cop, she reminded herself desperately. She'd been sent to arrest him.

And he knew it. The little thrill of panic that coursed through her was becoming familiar. She knew he knew it. Why else would he be looking at her with that kind of bottom-line honesty in his gray eyes?

And yet he was holding her close, moving her to the slow, sexy beat of the song on the jukebox, exerting just the slightest pressure to pull her closer, arousing her with his touch.

His hand made languorous circles between her shoulder blades, where her bra strap would have been if she'd been wearing a bra. When he shifted his weight in time to the music, their bodies brushed together lightly, once, twice, and then again. It seemed she was having an effect on him too.

She stepped away from him, and Simon slipped his hand down to the bottom of her shirt. His fingers brushed the bare skin just above her cutoff jeans, then slipped underneath the waistband.

It was just his fingertips, she thought desperately. It wasn't as if he had his hands in her jeans. She wasn't about to lose her head, forget her mission, and abandon herself to wanton sensuality over a couple of caresses, was she? That little shiver of response was desperation. And outrage. She just needed to get control of the situation.

"What do you think you're doing?" she demanded, her voice breathy.

"Not much," he murmured, his tone seductive and intimate. "Dancing with you. To tell you the truth, it's what I'm thinking about doing that's really taking most of my attention, Cleo."

"I'm . . . ah . . . not sure that's a good idea, Simon."

"What? Telling the truth?"

"Well, actually, Simon . . ."

"I have the feeling, Cleo, that you're a woman who finishes what she starts."

For a brief panic-filled moment, nothing but the truth presented itself to her. "I do," she said, for want of a better answer.

"I thought so," Simon said.

He let their steps slow to a halt while she met the mesmerizing gray gaze and said absolutely nothing.

It was, apparently, the answer he was looking for.

He slipped his arm around her waist and walked her across the room toward the exit.

SIX

It wasn't going to happen, Simon realized as he turned off Broadway and onto the tree-lined street where his second-floor apartment was located. The erotic anticipation that was frolicking merrily along the primrose paths of his imagination wasn't going to make it to the woods.

They had a chaperon.

Nickel was sitting on the back stoop, his shoulders slumped, his eyes glued to Simon's car. He looked as if he'd been sitting there awhile, resigned and waiting for confrontation.

Simon sighed, rounded up his stray imagination, and glanced across the seat at Cleo.

She was staring at the teenager as if he'd

been conjured up out of some gambler's pipe dream and deposited on Simon's doorstep by his favorite bookie. Whether she'd called them or not, the cops were back, and they were Cleo.

"Simon?"

"Yes, Cleo?"

"Nickel is sitting on your back steps."

"So he is."

"But what's he doing there?"

"Waiting for us, I imagine."

"But—" She broke off, apparently deciding that her avid curiosity wasn't quite in Cleo character.

Simon gave her the benefit of one raised eyebrow. "I guess he decided the drainpipe route wasn't his style. Duplicity is hard on the wardrobe. You know, snagged pants, grass stains, that sort of thing."

She stared back at him a moment, then straightened her shoulders and flicked a stray lock of hair out of her face. "Then again, Simon, maybe it's not the duplicity that's hard on a wardrobe. Maybe it's just you."

Point taken, Simon conceded, albeit in silence. He got out of the car and started around to open the door for her, but before he'd reached her side, she was out on the pavement, her oversized bag over her shoulder.

Cleo was not going to be left behind. He'd never met a woman with quite so much bird dog in her personality. Nickel was, for all intents and purposes, a sitting duck.

He followed her toward the house and worked on getting his body to accept that nothing but his imagination was getting inside those short cutoffs, where the sweet curve of Cleo's backside was beginning to show through dangling threads.

Nickel was avoiding Simon's gaze, shooting him a couple of guilty looks, and studying his feet. It was a measure of his dejection that one of his snazzy sneakers had a pigeon dropping on the toe. Nickel hadn't even bothered to wipe it off.

Simon stopped on the bottom step, eye level with the teenager. "Nickel."

He nodded back, then flicked a glance toward Cleo. "Ms. . . . ah . . . O'Nile."

"You'd better come in," Simon directed.

Nickel got up and stood nervously, jiggling on the balls of his feet and wiping his palms on the back of his jeans, then followed them up the stairs to Simon's apartment.

Simon snapped on a lamp and dropped his jacket on one of the computer monitors in the living room. Cleo eased her bag off her shoulder, and Nickel did some more jiggling. No one made any move to sit down. For a moment the inevitable ringing of one of Simon's phones was the only sound, a sound Simon ignored. Then Nickel sighed eloquently and said, "I really messed up, huh?"

"Yeah," Simon said. "You did."

"I paid all the money back to the kids. I told 'em I wasn't doin' it anymore. I never really meant to get into—"

"What you meant to do doesn't mean squat, Nickel," Simon cut in. "You're old enough to take responsibility for your actions. And the consequences of them."

"I know, I know. I'm willing to take the consequences. I know—"

"You *don't* know. You didn't get just yourself into this. You got Ranger into it too. Not to mention the restaurant, the folks who work there, and me, for that matter."

"Oh, man, what do you mean?"

"The cops are shaking your uncle down for protection money because the word's out you're making book in the Temple Bell,

Nickel. What kind of position you think that puts him in?"

Nickel shoved his hands into his pockets. "Oh, jeez. I'll pay him back. Somehow. I'll work for the money. . . ."

"Yeah, you will. But that won't necessarily fix things, Nickel. Sooner or later, when some crooked cop needs a bust to make his record good, who do you think he's going to go after? You know what happens to Ranger if he gets convicted again?"

Nickel stopped jiggling and sank down on the chair behind him, elbows on the armrests, head in his hands.

"You working for someone, Nickel?"

The boy glanced up, surprised, then shook his head. "No. It was just a couple of bets, you know, some kids at the school. It wasn't really making book, it was—" He broke off, catching Simon's expression, and recanted. "I guess it was, huh? But I wasn't . . . like working for a bookie."

"So who tipped off this cop that you were in the business, Nickel?"

"In the business?" Nickel repeated, clearly appalled. He had the confused, miserable look of the badly conscience-stricken. Simon folded his arms across his chest and waited. "I don't know, man. I wasn't talkin' to bookies or anything."

"You didn't have to. The word's out anyway."

"Is something going to happen to my uncle?" Nickel asked dejectedly, looking at his shoes.

"I don't know, Nickel."

Nickel stifled a moan, then ran his fingers through his hair, and finally met Simon's eyes. "So what should I do?"

More to the point, what should Simon tell him, with Officer O'Nile of the Saratoga police force listening in?

He glanced toward her. She'd made herself unobtrusive, leaning against the corner of a window frame, gazing down at the street, but he didn't harbor any illusions that she wasn't paying attention.

He'd figured it didn't make much difference up to this point. She'd known Nickel was guilty already, but so far she hadn't acted on it. He had to assume she was holding off to see how this thing shook down.

As if she sensed him watching her, she turned her head.

Her expression was thoughtful, direct, and easy to read: *Your move.* And if he called it right, she'd bend the rules enough to let him play this one out. He knew it with as much certainty as if she'd put it in writing. He just had to trust her.

He glanced back at Nickel, took a deep breath, and ignored his accelerated pulse rate. "You should apologize to your uncle, for starters," Simon said. "And offer your services as a dishwasher for as long as it takes to cover the expense you've caused out of pocket. Tomorrow I'll find out who gave you up to our local cop. With any luck, I can put some pressure on your snitch, make him give me names and dates and amounts I can take to the police. Maybe I can negotiate a deal that will keep your uncle—and you, for that matter—out of jail."

Nickel looked up, a ray of ever-optimistic hope glimmering in his eye. "You mean the cops don't have to know about it?"

Simon sighed. "Take my word for it, Nickel. Sooner or later you have to deal with the cops. In this case, it's going to be sooner."

Nickel's teeth worried his lower lip. The question was clear: *How much sooner?*

The answer was a little more obscure, depending as it did on the decision of Simon's "masseuse."

She was watching Simon, her arms

folded in front of her, her dark eyes serious. The come-hither flirtation had been replaced by an expression he hadn't known he wanted until he saw it in her eyes: approval. The kind of street-wise, savvy respect they both understood, from two different sides of the street.

"Why don't you go talk to your uncle, Nickel?" she said, startling them both. "And let Simon worry about the police."

"Oh. Ah . . . yeah. Good idea. I should do that." He stood up, and shoved his hands into his pockets. "Yeah. That's a good idea . . ." Nickel trailed off, his voice going absent, his gaze flicking back and forth between Cleo and Simon. "Well," he said finally. "I guess you two want to be alone, huh? So I guess I'll be going." He moved a step closer to the door. "I guess I'll go talk to my uncle."

No one answered him. Nickel sighed deeply and backed toward the exit, keeping his eyes on the two of them until he let himself out and shut the door carefully behind him.

Simon didn't have the damnedest idea what was going to happen next. This whole unlikely drama was totally nuts, he told himself, squeezing his eyes shut and taking in a deep breath through his teeth. He was in cahoots with the cops on a case he didn't understand. He didn't have any guarantees that he wasn't going to end up in the slammer, and his imagination was fixed unrelentingly on Cleo's cutoff jeans.

It wasn't going to happen, he repeated again. She wasn't even making a show of the masseuse act. She was standing still, her arms still crossed, the yellow glow of the lamp illuminating small, strong planes of her face. Her expression was open, readable, intelligent, and when she spoke, there was a quality of sincerity in her voice he couldn't doubt. "You handled that pretty well, Simon," she said softly.

"It wasn't unexpected. I kind of figured he'd be back here sooner or later."

"I guess you were right."

"Yes."

"He answers to you, doesn't he?"

"Yeah."

"Why you?"

"I got out of the slammer before Ranger did. I looked the kid up. He was living in a foster home, having a rough time. He needed some pressure to stay in school, a little push in the right direction—and he needs to stay out of the system."

"Meaning you want to keep him away from the cops," she said levelly.

"He's not a bad kid."

"I can see that."

She uncrossed her arms, rubbing her neck with her fingertips. "You're really going to talk to some . . . informant tomorrow?"

The light of the single lamp cast her body in clearly defined shadows: the straight line of her back, the athletic grace of her legs, the delicate curve of her unconfined breasts beneath the shirt, where her raised arm pulled the material taut.

He nodded. "At the track. You want to meet him?"

Her hand trailed down over the front of her collarbone, the gesture cautious, undecided, and sexy. "Yes," she said.

Simon felt all the nerve endings in his body stand at attention. *Yes.*

For some reason he couldn't fathom, Cleo minus the little catch in her voice was even sexier than she'd been playing the private masseuse act. He'd been right about her the first time he saw her. The kind of woman who would stand by her man once she made up her mind to have him. Tenacious, stubborn, loyal, strong—and woman enough to raise his temperature a few degrees with a single ambiguous *yes*.

"Okay," Simon repeated. He had an impulse to cut through the charade and tell her to level with him, lay out the truth, and let the repercussions fall.

He quelled the urge. An undercover cop whose cover was blown didn't usually get to hang around and see how things shook down. If his guess was anywhere close to right, the chief would demand an immediate arrest—Simon's—and listen to explanations later. He and "Cleo" were stuck in their respective identities until further notice.

There was no particular reason that should have bothered him as much as it did.

"Fine," he said. "I'll introduce you. Tomorrow."

"All right." She made another little gesture with her fingers, tracing the open placket of her shirt.

"I assume, then"—he glanced down at the bare hardwood floor, then back up at her—"that you're staying the night."

She didn't answer him. He didn't really expect her to.

He didn't want her to. If she said something, he realized, the insight taking him, it would be *no*.

She wasn't cynical enough to coolly agree to spending the night with a man she'd spent the day lying to.

And she didn't have any choice about lying to him. She was a cop.

A cop, he told himself, trying it out to see if the shock value still had any effect. Not much.

She was trying to arrest him, Simon reminded himself.

She'd lied to him, stolen his address book, cost him three hundred dollars, and damn near busted one of his best sources.

He couldn't think of anyone he'd rather haul off to bed and make love to until her toes curled.

She was looking around the place as if to assess its value for a night's lodging: bachelor pad, no visible guest bedroom, lumpy sofa . . . Simon. Her eyes came back to him, wary and more vulnerable than she had probably intended him to see. He had the impression her own home—not to mention her life—was a little more rule-bound than his.

So do something to really shock her. Be polite.

"Would you like something to eat?" he offered.

"I beg your pardon?"

"Food, Cleo. Are you hungry?"

She smoothed a strand of hair up into her ridiculously cascading ponytail, then wrapped her hand around it and hung on as if it were an anchor. "Starving," she said, the word a little bemused.

"Eggs, peanut butter sandwiches, or leftover Chinese?"

Her smile was restive. "I'm big on leftovers."

He indicated the kitchen, visible through the doorway. "You can have the run of the refrigerator."

He watched her consider her options: stay, leave, forget about being a cop, see the thing through to the end. Stick it out.

She let go of her ponytail, stretched a little taller, squaring her shoulders, then walked by him toward the kitchen.

Watching the back of her bare thighs moving with steady, determined steps toward his refrigerator, Simon sucked in a breath of sharp, sexually charged admiration. Most of the women he'd known would have run for the hills long before they'd come so far. This game of cops and robbers wasn't for the faint of heart.

But then, his Cleo wasn't faint of anything.

He should have known she wouldn't wait for him to open the refrigerator door for her. She was peering into the shelves, bending to see what he had on the lower levels, when Simon reached over her shoulder and took out a couple of white cartons. "Leftover Chinese," he offered.

She straightened, brushing his sleeve, caught between the refrigerator and Simon. The kitchen was in darkness, the two of them lit starkly by the rectangle of light— no secrets, no romantic candlelight.

A man, a woman, and leftovers. She took one of the cartons out of his hands, opened it, and sniffed. "Sweet and sour chicken?"

"Right." He stepped back, let her close the refrigerator door.

Cleo yanked open drawers until she found a fork. She speared a piece of chicken and put it in her mouth. "Good."

"I could heat it up in the microwave."

She shook her head and stabbed another piece of chicken. "Long as it's been cooked once, that's good enough for me."

His mouth curved in a slight smile. "Not a sushi fan, huh?"

She said nothing for a moment, eating

his leftovers. "My mother died when I was little," she said finally. "Before she died she taught me to cook. She didn't want my father and brother to go hungry."

"So you were the designated cook because you were the girl?"

She shrugged. "I didn't mind. It was a way to help. My dad worked long hours, and odd shifts sometimes."

"What did he do?"

Cleo studied the carton, then let the fork drop back down into it. "He was a cop."

Simon nodded, his gaze level, then said, "Let me guess. You didn't mind doing the dishes, but you hated being left behind when he went out fishing or playing baseball or mowing the lawn with your brother."

"That's pretty good. You tell fortunes too?"

"The future's a little harder to read," Simon said.

She let out a breath, smiled fleetingly, and went back to her food. Halfway through the carton, she glanced up at him. "Do you want some?" she asked as if it had just occurred to her that she was the only one eating.

"No, thanks."

"Mmm." She nodded, put another piece of chicken into her mouth, but stopped chewing when she caught him staring at her. She looked away, but he couldn't miss the nervousness in her eyes.

She finished chewing, swallowed, smiled. "This is really good. Where's it from?"

"Denise's."

"Mmm. Never been there."

"Any weekday afternoon, it's a good place to find a bookie."

She stopped again, fork halfway to her mouth, set the carton down on the counter, and reached for the one Simon still held. "But I don't need to find a bookie, Simon. I already have. A couple, in fact."

"Mmm. The question is, what are you going to do with them now that you've found them? That's moo goo gai pan," he added helpfully as she opened the box.

He'd moved, without really meaning to, a little closer to her. She glanced up at him guardedly, keeping the fork between them. "I know."

That fascinating husky note was back in her voice.

"Interesting question though, isn't it? What next?"

"Simon . . ."

"We never did finish that dance, Cleo."

She put the fork into the carton and carefully inched away from him on the pretext of setting it on the counter. Simon reached across the counter to switch on the radio and fiddle with the dial. The sound of a slow, sensuous saxophone floated out of the small speaker. Simon's hand brushed her arm as he straightened.

She tipped over the carton and the fork clattered into the sink behind her. "Oh, my."

"Don't worry about it."

"No. No, I won't."

He stepped close enough to touch the shoulder of her shirt in a gestured invitation to dance.

"I mean yes," she said hastily.

"Yes?" Ignoring logic, not to mention Cleo's body language, he let his hands gently caress her back.

"No. Yes. I mean—" She raised her hands between them, palms out, then clasped them together in front of her chest.

"Well," she said breathlessly. "This is an

opportunity for us to . . . ah . . . get to know each other, isn't it?"

He had the strong impression she wasn't referring to the particular way he had in mind. He raised an eyebrow. "What do you want to know?"

"Oh—you know—odds and ends." She shrugged and waved a hand. "Hobbies . . . birthdays . . . favorite movies . . . fundamental moral beliefs."

He considered for a moment. "Reading, October fifth, *No Mercy*—the one with Richard Gere and Kim Basinger, lapsed Episcopal."

"Lapsed."

"Yeah. How about you?"

Her chest rose and fell. "Simon . . ."

"Cleo."

There was a short silence, charged with momentary consideration of the consequences, then she said softly, "It's Jo."

Simon's thoughts were momentarily thrown into disarray. "Who the hell is Joe?"

"I am. That's my name, Simon. My name is Jo."

"Jo?"

"That's right."

"Jo."

"And . . . I'm not really a masseuse. I've been—"

"Cleo."

"Ah . . . no. It's—"

"Jo. Right. I've grasped that, Cleo."

"And I'm not—"

"Yes," he said, cutting her off. "I've got it."

"You've got what?"

Simon let out a breath, pinched the bridge of his nose, and his body and his brain fought a short battle. "I think I've got the essentials, Cleo," he said finally. "And I think maybe we should leave it at that."

When he opened his eyes, she was looking at him with a troubled expression he recognized as conscience. His Cleo didn't like dishonesty. It was wearing on her. She said, "It's just that, essentially . . . I mean, actually . . ."

"Cleo, stop there."

"It's—"

"I know what it is." *He just didn't want to say it.* He didn't want to talk about it at all. What was the next step—would she admit to being a cop? And then what? Arrest him? Haul him off to jail?

Or—worse—quit the case, say *sayonara* and walk out without a backward glance.

In those shorts.

"Let's not get carried away with too much . . . ah . . . strict honesty, all right?"

She said nothing, looking at him with that shadow of guilt darkening her dark eyes. Simon felt another twist of emotion, right in the center of his chest, inconvenient and probably unjustified and mind-boggling in its impracticality.

This was not a good idea.

But maybe he could keep her from figuring that out.

"As opposed to unstrict honesty?" she asked softly. Her smile had enough mild panic to raise his temperature another five degrees.

Maybe they could dance in the kitchen to the music on the radio until he heard her make that little sigh in the back of her throat, and he slipped his hand into the waist of her shorts, and that knot in the front of her shirt came undone and he could just pick her up and carry her off to—

Simon gritted his teeth. The state he was thinking himself into wasn't conducive to dancing.

"Cleo," he muttered abruptly. "You have about five seconds to call the cops. Because the thing is, babe . . . there's absolutely no future in this."

He could have said it better, Simon decided, but he didn't need to. She got it. She knew as well as he did that "the future" was exactly as long as it took for her to admit she was a cop or for Simon to tip his hand about the anticop scam he was running on Ranger's behalf. And it would be even shorter if Nielson got any more greedy or stupid or desperate than he already was.

She stood absolutely silent, her arms crossed in front of her, her hands gripping her elbows, the pulse in her throat thrumming—fast enough to match his own.

Simon unclenched his jaw carefully. He wanted her enough to bend nails with his bare teeth, to leap tall buildings, to lock himself in the nearest jail cell and swallow the key.

"Look. Here's the deal," he told her. "You get the bed. I'll take the sofa."

She was worrying her lower lip with her teeth. "But . . . I'm not . . ." He could feel her voice getting huskier by the moment.

"Don't do that."

"What?"

"Make that sound in the back of your

throat. Not unless you want to dance, Cleo."

A flush of color crept up from the neckline of her shirt to tint her cheeks, and he caught the subtle, quick cadence of her indrawn breath. She felt it too, and Simon knew it: the heat, the pulse of arousal, the undeniable throb of ancient rhythm. The admission was in her eyes, some kind of soul-deep, elemental honesty that said too many of the things they shouldn't say to each other.

The music was still playing, issuing a nonverbal invitation. He made one last, heroically noble stab at common sense. "Good night, Cleo."

He made the mistake of meeting her gaze, the soft, dark brown eyes troubled, vulnerable . . . honest. "It's not Cleo."

Simon clenched his jaw again against the sound of need that wanted to come out of his throat. "No kidding," he muttered.

She unclasped her arms at the exact moment he reached for her, spanned her hips with his hands, and pulled her flush against him. He brought his mouth down onto hers, grasping the back of her head, taking advantage of her startled gasp to thrust his tongue into the soft, intimate recesses of her mouth. He turned his head to seal her mouth to his, to catch the soft moan that started in her throat, to eliminate once and for all, for what was left of the night, any possibility of talking.

He kissed her, long and hard and with primitive, demanding heat, claiming her with enough raw intensity to make them both dizzy.

When he realized she was clinging to him as if she couldn't stand up by herself, he broke off the kiss to slide his hands down over her backside and lift her up against him. She wrapped her bare legs around him as if she'd been doing that for years, as if they had the moves down to perfection, a sensual dance that was hot enough to drive him crazy.

"Simon," she breathed, breaking the no-talking rule, "where are we going?"

"This way," he said, walking toward the bedroom. "Follow me."

Technically, it was absurd. She wasn't following him, she was in front of him, pressed intimately against the zipper of his jeans in a way that sent bolts of sensation rocketing through his thighs, his legs, the pit of his stomach, with every step he took.

There was a phone ringing somewhere

in the apartment. Maybe two. Maybe all of them. The hell with it, Simon decided, kicking the bedroom door shut, leaning back against it, letting Cleo unclasp her legs and slide down the front of his body, feeling the pure sensual pleasure of friction.

The future could damn well call back later.

SEVEN

The bedroom door slammed, sending mild reverberations through Jo like aftershocks that raced across all the sensual nerves of her body. She was pressed against Simon, her breasts nestled against his hard chest, her hips locked with his, her legs corralled within the V of his thighs.

The thought that she was the woman he wanted and intended to have was unreal, thrilling, something out of a fantasy. Simon's bedroom was dark, and erotic, a forbidden place for scandalous abductions.

She wasn't sure a woman could be abducted, exactly, from the kitchen to the next room, but she was beyond splitting hairs. She needed—wanted—the fantasy: uncontrollable passions, her own surrender.

In the shadows, Simon's broad shoulders were just an outline against the door, his face an abstract study in the harsh masculine lines of desire. His hands roamed over her back in restless, seeking circles, stroking her shoulders, her ribs, the curve of her waist, her upper arms.

He'd kissed her, in the kitchen, with the kind of heat she could only have imagined before she met him, held her with the kind of trembling intensity that had left her breathless.

He was breathless too, she noticed, his chest rising and falling with the rapid cadence of his breathing. The sound was strident, needful, arousing in ways she didn't understand.

She shivered again, pressing closer to him, letting her eyes drift shut and her lips part in invitation.

There was a quality of unreality about the physical urges she felt, the urgency she sensed in Simon. It was like nothing she'd encountered before.

But the truth was, she wanted it. She'd wanted it in the kitchen, shivering from the cold of the open refrigerator and the heat of Simon's body. She'd wanted it all—the kiss, the heat, the abduction from the cold hard facts of who they were and why they were together.

There's no future in this, babe.

She couldn't deny it. But in some odd, crazy way, that desperate fact had pushed her into this.

A tremor of hunger and heat passed through her, making her hands curl unconsciously around Simon's shoulders. Stolen moments. Last chances. Reckless passion. Heat and desire. Simon's grip on her hips as he held her against him revealed all she wanted to know about the blatant state of his arousal.

She made a sound in her throat and moved just slightly, and elicited a stifled groan from Simon. The sound rippled through all her secret places.

"Don't do that, babe," he half groaned against her ear.

She pulled back, trembling, searching his face to see what she'd done wrong.

He groaned again. "Oh, God, no, don't stop. Don't—" He kissed her again, hard, then picked her up the same way he had in the kitchen, his powerful hands spanning her buttocks, and walked toward the center of the room. In the dark, his knees hit the edge of the mattress and they tumbled down onto it. Simon held her, then rolled her on top of him, his hands sliding beneath the back of her shorts. His palms were warm and hard against that sensitive part of her body, the frayed strings of her cutoffs tickling the undercurve of her buttocks with every slight movement of his hands, evoking little fuses of sensation all the way down her thighs.

She spread her knees and braced herself up on the mattress so she could touch him, her hands free to roam over his shoulders, his collarbone, the muscle-ridged chest, his flat stomach where his shirt tucked in.

She pulled it out, unbuttoning, pushing it aside, reaching for his belt buckle, abandoned and wild in her haste.

Simon unsnapped her jeans, unzipped them, and tried to lift her hips to drag her shorts down. But she wouldn't let go of his jeans, tugging, breathless.

"Lift up, babe," he rasped.

"You first."

"Okay. You Jane, me Tarzan. Go for it." He rolled over to accommodate her, pinning her to the bed amid her breathless laughter, stopping it with a kiss. She pulled his jeans down to his knees and pushed them the rest of the way off with her feet.

He moved against her, reaching above her head. She heard a drawer scrape, and Simon raised himself a little higher. His broad, sexy chest was directly above her face, his hips pinning her to the mattress. She pressed her lips against the center of his chest. By moving her head just slightly, she could contour the hard, toned muscles, take in the taste and texture of his skin. She touched him with her tongue and felt his hand tighten on her shoulder as a shudder coursed through him. His reaction thrilled her, made her feel wanton and uninhibited. He'd turned a little, rummaging in the drawer, and Jo slipped her fingers inside the elastic of his briefs, and then, boldly, without a second thought—without even a first thought—touched him intimately.

The drawer crashed to the floor, spilling its contents all over the carpet. Simon swore, and Jo let go of him. Then, as if an afterthought, a glass rolled off the night table and smashed on the ground.

The seconds that followed were filled with heavy breathing and still-racing pulses. "Just looking for the condoms," Simon said apologetically, and reached over the edge of the bed. "Ouch, dammit!"

Reality was beginning to register in Jo's

sex-fogged mind. He'd cut his finger. Probably not on a condom. She peered over the edge of the bed into the pitch blackness, and Simon sighed and turned on the light.

They both leaned over the bed, staring at the litter on the floor. Broken glass, paperback books, pencils, a miniature tape recorder, a can opener, a stray button, and a desk lighter. No condoms.

Simon looked back at her, gave her a wry grin, and sat up. "I must have left them in the bureau."

He scooted off the bed, nimbly avoiding the contents of the spilled drawer, and pulled open the top drawer in the bureau.

Jo sat up slowly, leaning on her braced palms and willing her heart to slow down.

Her gaze wandered around the room, taking in the framed photos on the wall, the neatly filled bookcases that contrasted with the untidy piles of clean laundry cluttering various corners and surfaces.

The shadows had been chased by electricity, her abductor was searching through his bureau drawers for condoms, and without the sweet distraction of Simon's body pressed against hers, it was beginning to dawn on her that Jo O'Neal didn't do this sort of thing.

She sat dangling her legs over the edge of the bed and noticed she was still wearing her sneakers.

"Simon . . ."

"Mmm?"

"Simon, maybe this isn't . . ." She stood up, crunching on the glass underneath her feet.

Simon stopped what he was doing and turned around.

She avoided his eyes and zipped up her shorts, trying to look casual.

"Oh, babe, no . . ." He took a step toward her and circled her waist coaxingly. "Come on over here and help me look, okay? Just stand right here."

She took two reluctant steps, and he eased her in front of him and reached around her to pull open another drawer. He nuzzled her ear. "Just don't move for a moment, babe. Just stay . . ."

A tickle of sweet, sizzling sensation made its way down the side of her neck, followed by a tickle of panic. She could feel him against her backside, still blatantly aroused, erotically masculine, compelling her thoughts in a single dangerous direction.

Another shiver of panic jolted her, traveling directly up her spine from her tail-bone. "Simon, I don't think we should be doing this."

"Shh . . . don't say that."

"Maybe not finding them is a sign, Si-mon. Maybe it means we should . . . I mean, shouldn't . . ."

His drawers were a jumble, the bureau a mess, laundry scattered on the chair. How he could find anything in this—

She spotted the cardboard box on the floor not far from her foot at the edge of the bureau. Little foil packages spilled out of the open top.

On an impulse driven by the sudden un-expected deliverance that fate had offered, she kicked the whole collection under the bureau and out of sight.

"I guess they're not here," she chirped breathlessly, glancing at him over her shoul-der.

"Yeah. But where would they go?"

"You used them all?"

He frowned at her. "Sweetcakes, if I had used a whole box of condoms, I think I would have remembered it." He scanned the bureau again.

She inched away from him, stepping on a stray foil packet. She looked up in time to meet Simon's gaze. "Maybe they're in the bathroom," she suggested, moving another inch away from him, her hands behind her gripping the edge of the bureau. "Did you look in the bathroom?"

Simon stared back at her, gray eyes wary, one eyebrow raised in a skeptical expression. "No, I didn't look in the bathroom."

She lifted her hands in front of her, palms toward him. "Simon."

He took in the gesture, her defensive posture, and sighed deeply. "My guess would be that I can stop looking, huh?"

She let her hands drop, clasped them in front of her, reached for the bureau again, then crossed her arms in front of her.

"So . . ." she began self-consciously, "how come you never put your laundry away?"

"Sometimes I do." His mouth quirked up at one corner. "But then I can never remember where to find my underwear."

She cleared her throat. "You're wearing your underwear, Simon. In fact, that's just about all you're wearing."

"Do you want me to take it off?" he inquired, then sighed again. "Guess not." He picked up his jeans where they'd been tossed, and pulled them on. He was wearing one sock. He pulled it off by the toe and flung it toward the clothes hamper in the corner.

Three-pointer.

He fetched a dustpan and brush from just inside the bathroom door and swept up the broken glass beside the bed, dumping it into the wastepaper basket.

He straightened, frowned at Jo, then walked toward her, dustpan still in hand. "You don't do this sort of thing often, do you?"

"I guess that depends on what you mean by often."

"About as often as George Foreman fights Mohammed Ali, huh?"

She had no idea how often that particular event occurred, but she wasn't about to argue. She nodded.

"Thought so," Simon commented.

She glanced around the room and stopped on a black and white, formal publicity photo of Ranger in boxing gloves and shorts, smiling at the camera. His signature and a greeting to Simon were scrawled across the corner. "Did Ranger teach you to box?" she asked.

"No." His mouth quirked again. "He taught me to fold laundry."

"Laundry?"

He nodded.

"He was halfway through his sentence when I went into the slammer. He knew all the ins and outs. Folding laundry according to regulations was a particular passion of one of the less friendly guards."

"Oh."

"Yeah."

"That's why you don't fold it now."

He smiled briefly, glanced down at the dustpan and brush in his hand, bent to set them on the floor, then leaned against the bureau, beside her. "Jo," he said. "So what's it short for? Josephine? Joanna?"

"Mary Jo."

"Mary Jo? After the Holy Family?"

She smiled. "No. After my mother's younger sister. The black sheep of the family. In the hope she'd give up her wild ways and agree to be my godmother."

"Did she?"

"No. She ran off with an accountant who was laundering money for the mob and ended up in Scarsdale with an Olympic-size pool and a maid."

"Mmm." The sound was impressed.

"The black sheep in your family do it up right. All I did was become a lapsed Episcopal and give up playing tennis."

"And go to jail."

His smile acknowledged she had a point. "Well, yeah. That too."

"You got sent up deliberately, didn't you?"

He hesitated, then nodded at her.

"Why?"

"I was following a story and I didn't want to let it get away."

"So you went to jail for six months? Just like that? To get a story?"

"Uh-huh."

"You don't know when to quit, do you?"

He turned toward her, his weight leaned on one hip, his arms crossed in front of him. "I have a feeling you can relate to that particular quality."

He was standing close enough to touch, his shirt hanging open over his bare chest and his briefs.

"Was it worth it? To get your story?"

He shook his head. "No, but it was the story of a lifetime, or so I thought."

Jo let go of her elbows and let her hands fall to her sides. She couldn't take her eyes from him, his long hair, the coiled strength in his boxer's body. The defiant challenge in his stark independence. The cool, intelligent gray eyes that could hold an empathy that startled her, emotions that took her breath. That wry grin with its unexpected hint of self-deprecating humor. The ruthless, principled demand for honesty.

"Mary Jo," he said, the words a rough, soft murmur.

Her smile was edged with panic as shivery and sensual as night wind. "That's right. Nothing exotic."

"Pretty," he said.

Something about the tone of his voice made her breath catch. "Pretty?"

He raised his hand to her face and brushed the edge of her jaw with his fingers, feather-light, just barely touching her. "Strong. Straightforward." He touched the base of her chin, a faint gossamer pressure lifting her face to his. "Sexy."

He lowered his mouth to hers slowly, making her heart pound. Then touched her lips with his gently, lightly, in a lazy brush of a kiss that could have been sweetly innocent but for the hot, sensual flood of emotion that burgeoned forth from Jo's innermost places. Her lips parted, her hands moved to his waist, her resistance melted and flowed away like warm honey.

Simon raised his hands to circle her face and kissed her left eyelid, then her right, while she waited for his kiss, wanting it. He hovered, not moving, his breath warm on her forehead, then, with that same mesmerizing slowness, threaded his fingers into her hair. He worked his fingertips under the elasticized ruffle holding her ponytail, then drew it off carefully. Her hair fell loose, and Simon's fingers combed through it again as he bent his head to kiss her.

Reason, logic, self-protective instinct fled as Jo gave herself up to the kiss. Simon's strong hands cradled the back of her head, caressed her neck, palmed her shoulders, and then closed around the sleeves of her shirt, gripping her arms, bringing her body against his.

The foil packet crinkled under her foot, and she took a step closer, leaning against him with the top of her body.

Simon stopped kissing her to stare at the floor. One eyebrow rose and he gave her a slow smile of disbelief and admiration. He picked up the condom, fished the box out from under the bureau, then slipped his hand around her neck and kissed the bridge of her nose.

"Tell me, Mary Jo," he said, "do you like making love with the lights on or off?"

"Off."

He nuzzled her ear, then touched his tongue to the cord of her neck just below her jawline. When she shivered in response, he did it again. "Music?" he murmured.

She nodded.

His mouth moved back to hers and touched her lips. "What kind?" he said against her mouth.

"Motown."

His mouth moved over hers, forming patterns, soundless words, sensual explorations. "Okay."

"The call numbers are—"

"I know."

He walked her toward the bed, controlling her movements with his own. She felt as if her own will, her own desires, were the force that got them to his bed, where he laid her down in the circle of his arm. He leaned above her to turn on the radio on the night table. Something sweet and vocal filled the room, and Jo's senses as well, the rhythmic, hypnotic music stoking her emotional responses like Simon's slow, expert caresses.

"Covers or not?" he muttered, the words barely distinguishable with his lips pressed against hers.

"Just the basics." The words were indistinct, but he caught her meaning, ripping open the foil packet with three fingers.

"You know," he told her, his hands unbuttoning her shirt, "you could have just said no."

"No," she teased him, delighting in the intoxicating sense of power his arousal gave her. "I couldn't."

He laughed, his breath warming the sensitive skin above her stomach. Waves of sensual awareness pulsed through her, turning her body to molten lava: hot, elemental, eruptive.

He moved above her, pulling their bodies together while he switched off the lamp.

His hips urged hers to match his rhythm, building on each thrust until she moved with him in ancient primitive motion, underlined by the beat of the music.

Still moving slowly against her, he braced himself above her, searching her face by the dim light that filtered through the windows. Then he clasped her head in his hands while his gaze caressed her face, her neck, the wedge of skin that showed above the second button of the shirt she wore.

"Unbutton it for me, Mary Jo," he commanded, the words rough with emotion.

She didn't need much urging. Her trembling fingers found the buttons, opening them, inviting his touch, his mouth. And his mouth was there, hot, wet, yearning, pressed against each slowly revealed inch of skin.

Jo's fingers hesitated, paralyzed by the sensations he elicited with his lips and tongue.

Lost in desire, she rolled over and settled on top of him, running her hands across the muscles of his chest, pressing her mouth against the pulse at his neck. As she explored and admired the hard, honed ridges of his body, Simon undressed her, easing the shirt over her shoulders. His fingertips traced the outline of her torso to her breasts, and then along the undersides, until she arched into his hands, inviting his touch with her body.

Simon flipped them over again and dipped his head to her nipples while his hands tugged off her jeans, uncovering her at last. He joined their bodies slowly, by exquisite inches, inexorably making physical the emotional link that held them in thrall to each other.

A groan escaped from her lips. "Yes, Mary Jo," he murmured in her ear. "Tell me. Tell me what you want."

Freed by the force of Simon's passion, she told him in words and sounds he drew from her throat as his skillful hands shaped her breasts, warm on her bare flesh.

Jo mimicked his motions, exploring skin and muscle, molding the contours of his body above hers, delighting when he shuddered at her touch.

Trembling, denying the hot, raw rhythm that compelled him to move, he stopped, hovering above her, searching her face. On the radio, a rough emotional voice crooned about what happened when a man loved a woman, listed the ways he defied the world for her, confessed the risks he took to keep her.

With agonizing control he drove into her again, speaking in a language she'd never before understood, taking her with him to a place she'd never thought to claim. She clung to him with abandon, her breath coming in gasps.

"Oh, God," he whispered, "you're beautiful . . . Cleo . . . Jo . . . sweetheart."

She was, she thought. He was. They both were. They were right together. Simon's hand slid again to the back of her head, turning her toward him, kissing her nose, her eyes, her mouth, coaxing open her lips, his tongue slipping inside her, moving to the rhythm of their bodies.

His hands trailed down her sides, her hips, and lifted her thighs for deeper penetration as the tremors of response started within her.

Her hands clutched at his shoulders, her back arched, her heels pushed him closer. He felt connected to her heart, her breath, the center of her femininity. They rode it together, joined together. The world fell away as Simon's soul blended into hers, driving her, beat for beat, until they exploded on the sweet, sweet transporting wave that dissolved all her former notions of herself as a lover and a woman.

And a cop.

It didn't matter who she was, who he was. Only that she was his and he was hers, body and soul.

EIGHT

Sunlight was streaming into the room when Jo awoke to strange scraping, rustling noises. She made a small, startled sound and sat up, momentarily disoriented. Pulling the covers to her chin, she turned toward the sound. Mice? Squirrels?

A naked man?

Yes, there was a half-naked man in the room, his back to her, rummaging through the bureau drawers.

"Simon?"

He straightened and turned around to look at her. His hair was wet, dripping onto his shoulders and bare chest, and he was wearing only jeans, zipped but not snapped.

"Yeah. It's me."

So it was. Simon Faro. In the flesh.

A rivulet of water trickled down his collarbone, angled across the center of his chest, and ran between the sculpted pectoral muscles.

He shifted his weight, bringing her attention to the long legs inside the jeans, the angular joining of hip and thigh where she'd had her hand, her mouth. Incredibly sensual. While Simon's hands on her body were—

The hands in question appeared in her line of vision, snapping the waistband of his jeans. Jo lifted her eyes hurriedly to his face, feeling heat flood her cheeks.

He was smiling, a satisfied man, his gaze flickering over the sheet that covered her. "You were expecting someone else?" he asked.

She could feel her own smile straining around the edges. "Er . . . no. No, of course not."

Of course not, she repeated for her own benefit. She was, after all, in Simon Faro's apartment. In Simon Faro's bedroom. In his bed, in fact. Who else would she expect to come wandering in, half naked, with water dripping down his chest?

"Are you all right?" Simon asked softly enough to make her look at him again. He was frowning, concern in his eyes. "Jo?" he said.

Jo.

She felt a tendril of heat uncurl deep in the center of her body. Something fragile, trusting . . . and crazy. He had only to say her name and her wall of defenses collapsed into a pile of rumpled bed sheets around her toes. *Jo. Mary Jo.*

He knew who she was. They both knew. Oh, God, what was she doing here? An alarming, slightly belated buzz of panic shot through her.

"Of course I'm all right. Why wouldn't I be all right? I mean, I'm fine."

She noticed his expression changed from puzzled to assessing. His gaze moved from her hands, clutching the sheet, to the bedside chair, where their shirts hung haphazardly from the seat.

"Fine," he repeated, a slight edge to his voice.

What would he have preferred, Jo thought. Ecstatically transported? On the verge of paralyzing anxiety? "Fine," she said once more.

He frowned at her again, as if wondering what he'd missed. "I took the first shower.

You looked like you wanted to sleep in. We didn't get much—"

"Fine," she said, cutting him off. "I'll take the second shower."

"Okay," he said. "I got out a new toothbrush. It's on the sink."

"I have a toothbrush."

He nodded, still staring at her. "Well, then—help yourself. I'm all done in there." He gestured toward the bathroom, then frowned again, when she made no move to get out of bed. "Do you need anything else?"

"Just waiting for you to leave," Jo told him.

"Why?"

"Because I don't have any clothes on."

"I didn't know there was a dress code."

"Simon . . ."

"Mary Jo."

Jo squeezed her eyes shut. His voice, when he said her name made her heart lurch painfully, as if something in Simon had connected to something in her. As if he could read her thoughts, feel her feelings. That wasn't possible, was it?

A rush of blood to her head made her feel faint. She suddenly felt a shaft of longing that horrified her. Surely she wasn't capable of becoming so emotionally involved in one passion-filled night. Was she?

"Maybe," she said carefully, not opening her eyes, "you should call me Cleo, Simon."

"Cleo?"

She nodded.

"*Cleo.*" He sounded as if it had about as much appeal as calling her Queen Victoria and dropping a curtsy while he said it.

There was short silence, then Simon asked, "You want to talk about this?"

Her eyes opened abruptly. *Talk about it?* Was he crazy? A convicted felon running a scam on the police department and a cop who was trying to arrest him? What was she supposed to do—read him his rights first?

He sighed, and pinched the bridge of his nose. "No," he said. "I guess we don't want to talk about it."

Simon stood for a moment, regarding her, then he took a couple of steps toward the doorway. "I'm making bacon and eggs," he said.

"Oh." She nodded. "Good."

"One egg or two?"

None, she thought. She was feeling a little queasy as it was. But she was desperate to have him out of the room and occupied with something other than her. Breakfast seemed the best alternative. "Two," she said.

He nodded again and walked out of the bedroom.

Jo let out a long breath. It wasn't like her. None of this was like her.

It had to be taking on a new identity. She'd gone too far, become Cleo, lost track of herself in the process. It happened.

But hearing Simon call her Mary Jo had made everything worse. None of it made any sense, Jo admitted with a little groan. She needed a cup of coffee, a long, bracing shower, and a grip on herself. Working from the back of the list, she rummaged in her bag for a clean T-shirt, bra, and panties and headed for the bathroom.

Simon was in the kitchen fifteen minutes later when she appeared in the doorway, dressed, including underwear, he noticed. She looked as if she were making a serious effort to avoid thinking about what they'd done the night before.

"Hi," Simon said finally.

She hesitated for a moment. "Hi."

"You found everything you needed in the shower?"

"I did, yes. It was—" She avoided saying *fine* again, probably sensing his reaction if she did. "You're making bacon and eggs," she offered.

"Yes. Are you hungry?"

"Oh, yes. Absolutely. Starved."

She was acting as if the only heat in the room were coming from the frying pan, Simon thought, irritated beyond any reason he could fathom. The truth, obviously, wasn't an option.

"Bacon and eggs coming up," he muttered. "Cleo."

She took the plate from him, careful not to make body contact with even the tips of his fingers, murmured a thank-you, and sat at the kitchen table.

Simon filled his own plate and took it to the table, along with the coffeepot and two mugs.

"Coffee?" he asked.

"Oh, yes. Thank you."

"Cream?"

"Yes, please."

"Sugar?"

"Thanks."

"A passionate early-morning tryst on wrinkled sheets?"

She froze with her coffee cup halfway to her mouth, shifted her gaze away from him, then looked back, her smile a little pained. "Just coffee, thanks."

"How about if I change the sheets?"

She went through the stalled coffee-cup routine again, then said, "Good idea. I'll wash the dishes."

More like wiping up spilled milk instead of crying over it, Simon surmised. He recognized the attitude. Morning after a major mistake. Belated recognition of doing something stupid. Reckless impulse. Bad bet. The only reasonable course of action was to write it off. Leave it behind.

It was his own personal philosophy, tested over a long and varied history littered with mistakes, but he didn't remember it ever causing his gut to knot and his chest to feel too tight.

A mistake. What she'd been doing all night was making a mistake. And it was Simon.

"Hey," she said, surprised. "This is really good."

Simon scowled at her. Whatever pangs her conscience was suffering didn't seem to affect her stomach. Apparently there was nothing like moral dilemma to work up an appetite.

Not to mention great sex.

She ate everything on her plate systematically and completely, and wiped up the egg yolk with the last bite of toast.

For a few seconds of awkward silence, they stared at each other over empty plates, knowing that the moment of truth was at hand.

The phone rang.

It was one of Simon's—still in his jacket pocket. He tracked it down to the living room, picked it up, and said, "Faro." Then, "Nickel?" Pause. "You've been what?"

Jo sat up straighter in her chair.

"No. Don't repeat it. Who was the arresting officer? Listen, Nickel, just sit tight. I'll be there in a few minutes."

His glance toward Jo said things she didn't want to hear. Quite a few of them.

"Don't talk to anyone without a lawyer," Simon instructed. He punched off the phone, put it on the counter, and shoved his hands into his pockets.

She didn't have to ask what had happened. Nickel had been arrested. The officer, she guessed, was Nielson. The question was what to do about it now.

Simon yanked open a kitchen drawer and got out his bankbook.

She stood up from the table and faced him. "I'll get him out," she said.

"What?"

"Nickel. He's been arrested, hasn't he? I'll go . . . bail him out."

He gave a huff of disbelief. "I'll go bail him out. You just—"

"Just what?"

"Simon, I could help. I mean, I could . . ." *Could get him off. Could pull some strings. Could be a cop.* She didn't say any of those things. "You could just let me handle it," she finished lamely. She could see the futility of her suggestions on Simon's face.

"Not a chance, sweetcakes," he said. He picked up his jacket and snagged the car keys out of his pocket.

"Simon—"

"Later."

"I'm coming with you."

Simon's nostrils flared as he took in a breath, then let it out. "Nobody who had ever met you, Cleo, would expect you to wait here."

She picked up her bag and followed him out the door.

Simon locked it behind her and helped her into the car before getting in himself.

"Simon—"

He gave her a look.

"I didn't have anything to do with Nickel getting arrested."

"Good," he said after a moment.

"Not that I know of anyway."

"There is that catch," he agreed, pulling out into the street.

"When did he get arrested?"

"About half an hour ago."

"What for?"

Simon turned onto Broadway, toward the police station. "He was returning some money to one of his former clients at Ranger's place."

"He was *returning* the money? Giving back the bet, you mean?"

"He was in the wrong place at the wrong time. That's basically what his crime was."

"Mmm," she said noncommittally. Then she added, "It was Nielson, wasn't it?"

"Yeah."

Nielson. Either he'd needed to make a bust to divert suspicion, or he'd been sending a message to the parties he perceived as a threat to his operations. Or both. Had he recognized her in Ranger's place?

Jo worried her lower lip and wondered how much of this bad luck for Nickel had been her fault, and why.

She knew it was a useless endeavor, but it was a diversion from the more damning question of whose side she was on in this convoluted, contemptible, career-snagging case.

She was a cop, of course. She knew what side she was on. She was on the side of law and order. Spending a night of unbridled passion with a man who consorted with bookies, harbored young criminals, and was collecting information for a damning denunciation of the Saratoga Police Department didn't enter into it, did it?

Maybe she should ignore that question for the moment, Jo decided. She was feeling a little queasy.

They lurched along through stop-and-go traffic. Broadway was clogged, as always in the August racing season, with more population than it was meant to handle. Simon didn't seem to have much patience for it, an attitude Jo wouldn't have attributed to him. He presumably loved the racing season, to judge from the topics of his articles. He clearly wasn't a bookie himself, but he certainly knew a lot of them. If he wasn't betting on the horses, what was the purpose of all those phone calls?

Unfortunately, the chief's suspicion came to mind. Simon was digging up dirt on the Saratoga Police Department. It wasn't going to be hard for him to put together quite a good-sized heap of it, including harassment of an innocent businessman and the probably unjustified arrest of his nephew. The force wasn't going to look like good guys.

The chief wasn't going to be happy.

Jo was probably going to be pushing papers in the basement filing room for the next thirty years.

"Simon," she murmured as they approached the station, "why don't I just run in and take care of this? I've got my checkbook, and I owe you a favor for bailing out my car. It won't take me a minute, and that way you won't have to worry about—"

Simon's hard-eyed look and tight-lipped grimace derailed her train of reasoning. He pulled into a miraculously available slot at curbside, and Jo finished lamely, "—about parking."

"Wait here, Cleo. If Nickel comes out before I do, don't run him down. If I come out first," he added, getting out, "don't run me down either." He started to walk away, turned back, and pulled the keys out of the ignition. "Don't go anywhere, Cleo. Around this neighborhood, you're liable to get arrested in those shorts."

Jo watched him jog up the steps as she sat fuming. Damn him, he was right about the shorts. She *didn't* want to go trotting into the station dressed like . . . Cleo.

She should have brought another pair of pants. Or a dress, or something. She didn't have enough . . .

She still had the phone though.

Thirty seconds later she'd been put through to the chief.

"O'Neal?" he said, sounding as if he hadn't quite swallowed his latest gulp of coffee.

She didn't waste time on niceties. "Simon Faro is at this moment walking into the station."

"You arrested him?"

"If I'd arrested him, I'd be walking in with him, Chief."

"Don't get cute, O'Neal."

She ignored the advice. "There's a minor glitch in the operation, Chief."

"What glitch?"

"Ranger's nephew has been arrested.

Faro is bailing him out. He's a juvenile, in for bookmaking, first offense, probably a trumped-up charge. Definitely won't stick."

"So what do you want, O'Neal?"

"I want him released in a hurry, Chief. Set the bail, get him booked, get him out. I don't want Faro spending too much time on this, getting distracted from his . . . pursuits."

The chief stopped mid-slurp again. "You're on to something, O'Neal? You got him nailed?"

"Not yet," she hedged.

"But you're getting close with this guy?"

The wording took her aback for a few seconds. Was she getting *close* with this guy? "I may need another night or two." She smiled at the double meaning.

A lengthy silence followed her statement. Then she heard what sounded like a horned toad with hiccups. The chief was laughing uncontrollably.

"You mean our boy"—hep, hep, hep— "fell for the oldest trick in the book?"

"That's not what I—"

"You mean ol' Slippery Simon Faro was actually faked out by his own—"

"I didn't say that, Chief."

"By God, it gives new meaning to the

word jailbait, doesn't it?" Hep, hep, hep, hep. "If I had it in the budget, I'd give you a raise, O'Neal."

"I appreciate the thought," Jo said with pained irony.

"I like your style, O'Neal. Remember to tell me what his face looks like when he finds out he's been—"

"Just get the kid out of jail for me, will you, Chief?" Jo put in. "Pull a few strings and expedite this thing, okay?"

"Oh, yeah. Our boy really likes you, huh?"

Jo sighed. "Crazy about me," she allowed. She punched the disconnect button, tossed the phone back into the bag, and wondered if the outcome would have been more or less embarrassing if she'd trotted into the station in her shorts.

Less, she decided.

The basement file room, Jo thought gloomily, was beginning to look pretty good.

Simon and Nickel were out of the station house five minutes later, in what had to be the fastest bailout in Saratoga history.

"That was quick," she said as Simon got into the front seat.

"I'll say."

"I've been waiting right here, Simon," she said blandly. "I haven't left the car."

"So I see."

Nickel, crammed into the tiny backseat of Simon's bachelor special, murmured a good-morning to Jo and a jumbled collection of thank-yous to Simon.

"That's all right, Nickel," Simon said. He glanced across the seat again. "Cleo couldn't have done it better if she'd gone in herself."

"Huh?" Nickel asked.

No one answered him.

"The Saratoga police station," Simon said presently, pulling away from the curb. "Always full of surprises."

"You seem to have had plenty of experience with it," Jo said tartly.

He gave her an ironic grin. "I have a feeling I haven't even scratched the surface, sweetcakes."

"I do have a name, Simon."

"Oh, I know. You've even got a spare."

That didn't warrant an answer. Nickel was watching the two of them as if he were a spectator at a Ping-Pong match, biting his lower lip.

Jo couldn't quite, however, resist the

challenge. "Shall we try for a third?" she asked with a low, husky catch in her voice.

He glanced at her warily. "I don't know. Are we talking last names here, sweet-cakes?"

"Oh, man," Nickel said from the back-seat. "Are you guys getting married?"

The jag swerved toward the opposite lane, Jo shrieked, and Nickel grabbed for the handhold in the backseat before Simon recovered control of the car.

Jo pried her fingers off the dashboard and straightened in the seat.

"No," she said.

"We haven't discussed it," he said at the same time.

"Oh, yeah," the teenager said. "I understand. It's a little . . . ah . . ."

"Premature," Simon supplied.

Jo gave him a look of disbelief, and Nickel frowned from one to the other, then gave in to a sly smile. "Oh, man," he said, delighted, "I hope I didn't let some secret out of the bag here."

Nothing that wasn't already shared by the superintendent of the Saratoga police force, Jo thought, feeling a little thread of hysteria. At this rate, they might as well just go public and announce it at the afternoon's racing meet.

"Don't worry about it," Simon said under his breath. He turned his gaze back to the road, but she could see that his jaw was clenched.

He needed a masseuse. *She* needed a masseuse.

Make that a physical therapist.

No, make it a psychiatrist.

NINE

Simon made the turn around Congress Park toward the Temple Bell by ignoring the fact that the traffic light had already changed. Ranger was out on the sidewalk, arms crossed in front of his chest. He caught sight of them and raised an eyebrow, but otherwise made no sign of being surprised that they had Nickel back already. Simon pulled into the one available spot along the curb.

Nickel was pointedly avoiding his uncle's stony gaze. "Your car's still here, Ms. O'Nile."

So it was, Simon noted, though he guessed his notably silent passenger would be a little more pleased at that fact if the car hadn't been quite so obviously visited by

Nickel's pigeons. They'd left quite a bit of evidence behind.

She got out of the Jag, shut the door, and stared. "Oh, my."

Nickel climbed out behind her. "I guess that wasn't the best place to leave it."

"I guess not."

"I could wash it for you," the teenager offered. "What the heck. I'm already gonna spend the next couple months of my life washing dishes. Might as well wash cars too. And then you could put it around back where there aren't so many birds. I feed 'em in the front," he finished in apology.

"Around back of the Temple Bell?" She frowned, craning her neck to see where Nickel was pointing. "I don't think so, Nickel."

Simon stood in the street, hands in his pockets, watching them.

"Hey, why not?"

"Well . . ."

Because Nielson would probably run the license, and when he figured out who she was, there'd be some pretty spectacular havoc at the station house, Simon figured. She couldn't, however, say that to Nickel.

"Oh, hey, my uncle won't mind, you bein' Simon's fiancée and all."

"Fiancée?" Ranger repeated.

Cleo looked—uncharacteristically—speechless. Shocked. Appalled at the very idea.

Simon could have helped her out. Ranger's one-word question was Simon's cue to set the record straight. He opened his mouth to do just that, glanced from Ranger to Cleo—and felt that peculiar tight sensation in his chest. Yesterday she'd been draping herself around his neck, murmuring, "Simon darling, how can I repay you?" and today she had her shorts in a knot because some delinquent teenager with a romantic streak had figured they were engaged. Sex—fine. Marriage—forget it. He knew that the whole undercover act was some asinine invention of his old nemesis, the chief, but for some perverse and probably self-destructive reason, he didn't feel like going along.

Simon pulled his keys out of his pocket and reached for the door handle to the Jag. "I'll park in the back," he said. "And Cleo can have my space."

When he walked back around the front, they were chatting while Nickel moved her car. Ranger had uncrossed his arms, and his stony glare had softened to the kind of affable courtesy due to a fiancée.

Which was more than Simon could say for himself. Her back was to him, and the frayed threads of her cutoffs gave him a tantalizing view of her thighs and the curve of her bottom.

He hadn't touched her since they'd awakened. He understood the word *no* when it was delivered at several thousand nonverbal decibels. He'd gotten the message, but every time he looked at her, his body was putting up one seriously convincing protest against it.

The hell of it was, he couldn't argue with her. Making love to her had been a mistake. Making love the way they had—abandoned, wild, sensual, for half the night—had gone way beyond the pale concept of a mistake. He'd never in his life had trouble keeping his hands off a woman, but from the way he'd been obsessing about her, he didn't trust himself to get too close to her.

She was a cop, for God's sake, Simon told himself for the seventieth time in the past hour. There wasn't any getting around that. Or over, under, or through it.

He sighed, shoved his hands into his pockets, and watched his imagination conjure up another scenario where she'd let him thread his fingers through her hair, slip his hand around the back of her neck, tip her face up . . .

Nickel and Simon converged on them at the same time, Nickel politely holding Ms. O'Nile's keys. Simon took her by the shoulders, spun her around to face Nickel, and stood behind her, blocking the view of her tempting backside from young, not-so-innocent eyes.

"Simon?" she said with a little questioning lilt in her voice that went right through him.

"Your keys, Cleo," he said.

She frowned, took the keys from Nickel, then started to turn around again, but stopped when Simon's grip tightened on her upper arms.

Ranger grabbed Nickel by the ear. "Come on, nephew. Let's leave the happy couple to themselves. You've got some dishes to wash."

The two of them disappeared into the Temple Bell. Simon and Cleo watched them leave before Cleo spoke. "Simon?" Her voice was carefully polite, but with, he thought as his heart started to pound, a little hint of something breathless and constrained. "Are you planning to let go of me?"

He wasn't sure.

Well, of course he was sure, he told himself. He hadn't completely lost control of his hands, even when they were resting on her shoulders, absorbing the heat of her skin through the T-shirt, setting loose images of where else his hands had been on her skin, where else they could go from there.

"Simon!"

He let go of her.

"Thank you." She looked at him accusingly, waiting, he realized, for an explanation.

"Just keeping you respectable, Cleo," he muttered. "The view wasn't suitable for a seventeen-year-old."

"What view?"

"The back of your shorts."

She blinked, genuinely confused, then said blankly, "The back of my shorts?"

"What there is of them."

She regarded him as if she thought he'd completely lost it. "We're talking about a teenager who climbs down drainpipes from the girls' dorm windows like a cat burglar, and you're telling me he's going to get extraneous ideas from my shorts?"

"Just keeping things respectable," Simon muttered.

"Respectable?" Her voice rose. "What is the matter with you?"

Good question, Simon thought, and shoved his hands deeper into his pockets.

"We're in the middle of a neighborhood where people come either to make book, take bribes, or eat raw fish, and you're trying to keep things *respectable*?"

"Sorry," he said with a touch of irony she didn't seem to notice.

She glared at him, unmollified, brown eyes shooting sparks, tousled hair practically aquiver with emotion, facing him down with the kind of determination that wouldn't give an inch.

Simon felt the urge to kiss her.

"We do *not* have a respectable relationship, Faro. And get this straight. I am *not* your fiancée."

Simon frowned at her.

"Have you got that?"

He wasn't sure. But he was getting some insight into what this conversation, absurd even by Cleo/Simon standards, was all about. "Why?" he asked, trying to read her

face, but she'd clammed up all of a sudden,
her face closed and wary. "Have you already
got a fiancé?" The stab of pure, unadulter-
ated jealousy that shot through him at that
notion made his already overtaxed heart
skip a couple of beats.

"No. At least not—"

"Not anymore?"

She crossed her arms again, defensive, a
little uncertain. Obviously, he'd touched a
nerve. "That's right."

Not anymore since *when*? Since she'd
met Simon? Just how ex was this ex-fiancé?
Because there was no question about it, Simon decided. After last night, this guy was
definitely an ex. "Have you *told* this fiancé
he's been ditched?"

She blinked. "What?"

"Does he know the wedding's off?"

"Have I told . . . ?" Her hands slid off
her elbows as her shoulders dropped. "Oh,
yes, he knows, all right."

Simon felt a rush of relief. Jealousy was a
draining emotion. "I thought maybe it was
a . . . recent decision."

"You mean *last night*?"

"Yeah. Last night."

"You mean . . ." She looked at him in
disbelief. "You think I just met you, and we

happened to . . . spend some time together and and then we just . . ."

". . . Made love?" Simon offered.

"No." She stepped back from him and raised one hand as if to fend him off. "No. Last night was just . . . I don't know what you're supposed to call it these days. Just—"

"What do you mean 'what you're supposed to call it'?"

"Oh, I'm sure you have some locker-room expression that you—"

"No." He cut her off. "No, I don't have any locker-room expression for it. I spend most of my time staring at a word processor. When I'm not in the slammer," he added levelly. "You're the one who has the locker-room experience, it seems to me."

"I do not—" She folded her arms, then she said in a low voice, "It's part of the job."

Simon studied her averted face while a delivery truck turned onto the street and slowed in front of the Temple Bell.

"Was last night part of the job too?" Simon said finally. "Because there's no way I can believe that, Mary Jo."

"Cleo," she bit out, stubbornly refusing to meet the challenge in his words.

"Why don't I just go back to 'sweet-cakes'? At least I made it up myself."

"All right." Her cool, sarcastic tone matched his. "Then you could pass it on to the next—"

"The next what? The next *masseuse* dressed in spandex who follows me into a massage room? Or the next sprinter who knocks Nickel down and dazzles him into complete infatuation?" His voice dropped. "The next woman I talk to about being an ex-con? The next woman who understands the kind of world I live in? I've already found her."

"No. It won't work."

"Why not? Is it against some regulation, or something? No dating ex-cons?"

"Maybe it is! Some of us actually follow rules and regulations. Some of us believe in law and order."

"I believe in law and order."

"No, you don't. You do whatever you like."

On the street behind them, the delivery truck was idling at the curb, the driver peering out the window. "Hey, buddy, is this the Temple Bell?"

"You got it," Simon told him. "Deliveries around back." He turned to Jo again. "What do you mean—"

"You impersonate cops. You consort

with bookies. You even park illegally." She leaned toward him, eyes flashing, color high, passionate with frustrated outrage. "You can't just go around breaking rules, no matter how good it feels."

How good it feels. He knew what she was talking about. And the fact that she *was* talking about it sent a sweet, surging wave of heat through his body. For a second he couldn't think, dazzled by the sexiest woman in the world telling him how good it could feel. When he spoke, his voice felt rough in his throat, his breath a little short. "Why not, sweetcakes. Let's break a few rules. Let's just see how it feels."

"Because—" Her voice sounded a little breathless too, and Simon loved it.

His blood was racing, his heart pounding, his senses anticipating every nuance of connection suggested by the electricity in the air. "There are consequences, Simon. There are penalties. There are—"

"Yeah, well, whatever they are, they're worth it." He dragged her against him. Before he brought his mouth down onto hers, there was a crash: the unmistakable sound of crunching metal followed by breaking glass. Both of them stared toward the loading dock, where the delivery truck had just pulled in. Where Simon's car was parked.

Had been parked, Simon realized, hearing the delivery truck driver's string of curses that followed. Then he heard the restaurant's back door slam open and Ranger's more imaginative string of curses.

"Simon?" she asked, trying to see over his shoulder. "What was that?"

"I have a feeling it was the sound of penalties and consequences coming home to roost, sweetcakes."

"Penalties and consequences?"

"Maybe," he conceded, "you have a point."

The grassy, shaded, two-acre parking lot of the Saratoga Racecourse accommodated vehicles that ranged from luxury Mercedes sedans to college-student junker specials, but even in the eclectic mix, Jo's pigeon-dropping-covered Escort stood out like a sore thumb. The parking attendant gave them a look that needed no interpretation, then did a double take when Jo got out, showing quite a bit of long, shapely leg in the process. She'd traded in her shorts for one of Ranger's African-print tablecloths, knotted at the waist, and had borrowed a pair of unbelievably high-heeled sandals from one of the pool players in Ranger's back room.

The whole getup was sexier than spandex and more risqué than her frayed shorts, but technically it met the clubhouse dress code. She wanted "mobility," she'd explained breezily.

Simon didn't doubt her. She had that no-nonsense, determined look he was becoming familiar with. She intended to wrap up this case, pocket her information, and make tracks. Simon had a strong suspicion that given the opportunity, she'd ditch him before the final stretch, drop her alter ego like small change at a betting window, and be pinning on her badge before she left the premises. Alone.

She'd come too close to kissing him outside Ranger's place to keep up the blasé, ships-in-the-night routine she'd tried to adopt that morning. One good kiss would have had those ships docked side by side and probably in the same berth, and she was too honest not to admit it to herself.

She'd never admit it to Simon though. She'd been avoiding him for the past hour—

acting as if she'd never touched him, never kissed him, never slept in his arms.

The idea that she was planning just to walk out of his life, back into the Saratoga police station, and file him away with his mug shots had his guts twisted into knots. He couldn't decide if he was furious, frustrated, or falling in love.

Unobtrusively, he pocketed her car keys, ignoring his twinge of conscience. He'd already learned that when dealing with his Cleo, he needed all the advantages he could get.

She was looking around the park grounds with interest, inspecting the little knots of families setting up barbecue grills and lawn chairs in front of the television sets mounted on every handy tree. Simon doubted that their informant would be sitting on a picnic bench kibitzing and eating hot dogs with the kids. But if he was, the poor sucker wouldn't get a chance to take the last lick of mustard before Cleo had him spotted.

After that it would be no contest. One two-hundred-fifty-pound ex-bookie stool pigeon against Cleo's lithe, determined, saronged body—he'd put his money on the saronged body. The idea, in fact, had possibilities, Simon decided with another covert glance toward her.

Or maybe he'd just throw her over his shoulder, haul her out of the park, and abduct her.

He had a feeling she could sense his intentions. She hadn't been within touching distance since the Jag had been crunched. Abduction, he admitted reluctantly, probably wasn't an option. He had to come up with some other plan.

"You figure this informant will be hanging out in the clubhouse?" she asked, heading for the red-and-white-striped awning across the grounds.

"Could be," Simon said noncommittally. He knew exactly where their informant would be—at the far end of the bar in the clubhouse restaurant. Charlie-the-human-data-bank kept office hours there for the convenience of his clients. Simon had used him several times in the past for sticky research questions. Charlie sold top-shelf, reliable information for commensurate prices, and, like any good businessman, kept regular hours.

"Hot dog?" Simon offered. "Beer?"

"It's a little early in the day for drinking, isn't it? We just finished breakfast."

It was one-thirty, but Cleo was vigilantly holding lawlessness and disorder at bay. Simon grinned at her. "We got a late start. It was such a . . . long and eventful night."

"We're not going to talk about last night, Simon."

"You brought it up."

"I did not—"

"Cleo," Simon interrupted, "that policeman over by the parade ring is watching us. Maybe we should make more show of the happy-couple façade."

She glanced toward the uniformed cop, who, as luck would have it, was looking the other way. "Let him think you just lost a bet and can't afford to buy me a hot dog," she muttered, but didn't object when Simon took her arm and steered her toward the awning.

"To the clubhouse, sweetcakes," he said. "Try to look like my masseuse."

He tucked her elbow under his, laced their fingers together, and walked her across the lawn toward the potted geraniums at the clubhouse entrance. They should be able to spend an hour or two sitting together in some intimate little corner before he "found" his informant. Maybe she'd bring up the subject of last night again. Her pulse was racing already, wasn't it? If not, his was racing enough for both of them.

"Table by the window, sir?" the maître d' offered as they entered.

"Ah . . . no," Simon told him. "We find the races a little distracting."

"Is he here?" Jo asked once they were seated at a table near the bar, and had ordered two frozen fruit concoctions.

"Is who here?"

"Your informant, Simon. The man we came here looking for."

"Mmm."

She frowned at him. "You mean 'mmm' yes, or 'mmm' no?"

Simon reached for her hand. "Trust me, sweetcakes. We'll find him."

"Trust you?"

"Say that one more time, Cleo. Try it without the question mark at the end."

"Stop looking at me like that, Simon."

"Like what?"

"Like you're thinking things you're not saying. It's too intense."

"I am."

"Well, stop it." She pulled her hand away.

"That's the thing, Cleo," he said. "About thoughts. About imagination. Fantasy. Memory. Sensory memory." Under the table, he slipped his palm over her bare knee.

"Here you are, sir, madam," the waiter said, placing a tall pink glass in front of Cleo. He smiled faintly at Simon. "I trust you haven't found the races to be too much of a distraction, sir?"

He gestured toward the windows, where, Simon noticed for the first time, there was a subdued roar of the crowd outside, and a less subdued chatter of commentary from the well-dressed patrons gathered at the window, watching the race.

"Not until recently," Simon murmured.

The waiter placed another tall pink glass in front of Simon. "Sir, I believe your phone is ringing."

"Thanks." Simon pulled the phone out of his coat pocket.

"Yo, partner," Ranger's voice said. "Nielson's just been here. I think something's up."

"Like what?"

"He's been asking a lot of questions. I think he knows somebody's got his number.

You're one of the logical choices. Watch your back, he might be on your tail."

"Got it." Simon put the phone back in his pocket, and reluctantly removed his hand from Cleo's knee. He glanced surreptitiously around the room just in time to see Nielson walk through the door.

"What?" she said.

Simon sighed. "Don't look now, but Nielson has arrived. I think it's time to talk to our informant, Cleo."

Charlie was sitting at the end of the bar next to their table, as usual sipping a cup of coffee and watching the race on the video monitor.

"I heard Ranger's kid got in a little trouble," Charlie said, eyeing Cleo with professional interest. She was eyeing him back, Simon noticed.

"Yeah," Simon agreed.

"So what do you want to know?"

"I want to know who gave him up to the cops. Particularly the cop that has that beat covered. Nielson is his name."

Charlie blew out a breath and slid his gaze toward Cleo again. "Is this a party?"

"She's okay," Simon murmured. "She's my fiancée."

"No kidding. Congratulations."

"Thanks," Cleo said faintly.

"Yeah. Well. You see that guy in the corner? Talkin' to your boy Nielson? That's him. Don't all look at once, all right? I'll send you a bill," he called after their retreating backs.

"Simon? Do you know this guy?"

Simon nodded. "Ex-bookie. He's had a lot of trouble with the law. Probably about to get busted again when Nielson got his claws in. He'll go for the highest bidder. And I've got a credit card."

"They take credit?" Cleo asked faintly.

"Not literally."

"Oh."

Simon glanced at her. "Listen, sweetcakes. I need ten minutes alone with this guy."

"But, Simon—how are you going to get him alone?"

He glanced at her to see if she was sincere, then spelled it out. "You're going to distract Nielson."

"Me?"

"Yeah. Buy him a drink, wave at him across the bar, then disappear into the ladies' room and keep him waiting."

"Disappear into the ladies' room?"

"Trust me, sweetcakes. Women do it all the time."

"But what if he—"

"—Recognizes you?" Unspoken truths clicked into place without requiring particular explanation. "He won't," Simon assured her. "Not in that tablecloth."

"What's my sarong got to do with—"

"Believe me, sweetcakes, it has plenty to do with it. And if he lays a hand on you, he's dead meat."

For a few moments she didn't answer him. Then she muttered something he didn't hear, wandered toward the bar, and leaned over it, giving quite a few interested patrons a tantalizing glimpse of sweetly rounded backside. She spoke to the bartender, then gave an inviting wave toward Nielson and wandered toward the rest rooms.

Nielson stared in the direction of Cleo's exit for several moments before he walked over to the bar.

"Got a bet for you," Simon murmured to the deserted snitch.

"What?" the man muttered.

"Venetian Red in the sixth, to win."

"Huh?"

"You taking bets?"

"Yeah.

"Let's talk about it—over in the corner."

Simon led the way toward an unobtrusive spot near the viewing windows. He positioned them so that Nielson's snitch was hidden among the crowd but Simon had a view of the crooked cop at the bar.

"You're the writer, aren't you?" Simon's quarry asked.

"Uh-huh."

"I've heard about you. Did time, didn't you? Wrote that book about it."

"Yes."

"You got a reputation on the street. Straight-shooter. Man who knows how to keep his mouth shut when it counts."

"Yeah, I know how to do that." Out of the corner of his eye he saw Cleo emerge from the ladies' room. Nielson saw her too. She hesitated a moment, sizing up the situation, pretending to look for someone. It was a dicey situation—but his Cleo had instincts that didn't quit. Her gaze skimmed over him without any sign of recognition, then she looked at Nielson, gave him a sexy smile, and made her way toward him.

If he recognized her, Simon figured, she could claim to be off duty, enjoying the races like half the rest of the town, and buy at least a few minutes of Nielson's attention with cop talk. Clearly, though, that plan wasn't necessary. Nielson had the dazzled, fantasy-addled expression of a man confronted by a knockout woman.

Part of him wanted to walk over there and insert himself between Cleo and that creep before he got any ideas. Time, he decided grimly, to get down to business with the snitch and get this deal over with.

"I've got a tip for you," Simon said levelly, then paused long enough to make sure the man was paying attention. "Your partner—Nielson—is going down."

"What are you talking about?"

"Internal's already got him in their sights," Simon lied. "The good news is— any pressure he's putting on you is about to disappear. The bad news—"

"Yeah?"

"—Is Nielson, being the worthless excuse for a human being he is, will probably give you up." Simon waited for that to penetrate. He didn't have to wait long. The man evidently knew Nielson too well to doubt the prediction. His hand tightened around his beer mug, but he didn't drink from it. He looked like his stomach had suddenly started to hurt.

"On the other hand," Simon continued, "if you cooperate with me, I think I can see to it that your name stays out of it. You might still have a future around this town."

"How you gonna do that?"

"Same way I've always done it. You want references?"

The man stared at him.

Across the room, Nielson had moved a step closer to Cleo, picked up his drink, and was smiling into her eyes. If he touched her, Simon decided, he was road kill. He wrenched his gaze back to the snitch, who'd started to go pale and a little green around the gills. "Make up your mind," Simon told him. "This is a one-time offer."

Five minutes later Simon had the evidence he needed, and a clear map for his future.

The only thing missing was the woman at the bar, who was flirting and switching her weight from one hip to the other in a way that brought entirely too much attention to her tablecloth.

It occurred to him that this jealousy bit was not particularly professional, when Nielson looked up, and realized, with some kind of male mating sense, that there was another man staring at the woman he was trying to hustle.

Two seconds later Nielson was bearing down on Simon like a Sherman tank, with Cleo on his heels. The snitch faded into the crowd before Nielson got across the room, but not before the cop had seen him. Nielson's face was darkening with anger and suspicion as he pushed his way through the crowd toward Simon.

"What the hell do you think you're doing here, Faro?" Nielson demanded.

"Watching the races," Simon said blandly.

"I know who you are," Nielson accused.

"Likewise."

"I know what you're doing too, and you're not going to get away with it." He fumbled in his pocket, clumsy with frustrated anger.

"Hold it right there, Nielson," Cleo said.

The cop gave her a distracted glance and muttered, "I'll get back to you in a minute, honey. Just as soon as I make this arrest."

Honey? He was calling her *honey?*

"Dammit, Nielson," she said. "It's too late. Internal is on to you. You think arresting their primary witness is going to stop the investigation?"

"Not stop it," Simon murmured through a clenched jaw. "But it sure as hell will gum things up for a while."

Nielson was staring at Cleo in shock and belated recognition, his jaw hanging open, his expression outraged.

"You're not arresting him, Nielson."

"You gonna stop me?"

"Yes."

A police badge appeared in front of Simon's face, but it wasn't Nielson's. Cleo had beat him to it. "Simon Faro," she said, "you're under arrest."

Simon gave her a blank look. "What for?"

"Car theft," she snapped out, reaching into her bag and making clinking sounds. "Now, hand over my car keys."

It wasn't, Simon reflected as she snapped the handcuffs on his wrists, exactly the way he had planned to prevent her from walking out of his life. And he would have preferred to plant his fist in Nielson's face after that *honey* remark. But a man had to take his opportunities where he found them.

Nielson was sputtering as if he'd swallowed hot coffee. The crowd around them had already turned their attention to the next race. Simon's phone was ringing.

"Could you get that for me, sweet-cakes?" he murmured for Nielson's benefit.

Cleo fished the phone out of his pocket, clicked it on, and held it to his ear.

"I'll have to get back to you later," Simon said. "I've just been arrested. By my fiancée."

TEN

"You want me to do *what*?" Jo stared at the chief as if he'd grown another head.

"Interrogate him."

"Interrogate him?" Her voice squeaked in disbelief.

"He's in room two."

Jo crossed her arms in front of her. "I told you—I'm dropping the charges."

The chief shook his head. "No."

"We're taking this to court? Has everyone around here gone crazy?"

"No," the chief said. "We're making a deal."

Jo was temporarily silenced. "A deal."

"Yeah. We drop the charges, and Faro turns over whatever evidence he has to Internal. He won't write about it, and we cooperate on a future story he's working on. One where we come out looking like the good guys for a change. But he has a couple of conditions."

"What are they?"

"He insisted that you do the debriefing, O'Neal. After all, you were the arresting officer."

"Chief . . ."

"Room two, Detective." The chief gave her his notoriously insincere smile. "Bring him a cup of coffee, why don't you?"

Simon was facing the window, tipped back in his chair, typing on a laptop and wearing headphones. Jo slammed the door loud enough to jolt him into slamming down on all four chair legs. He grabbed the keyboard, just rescuing the laptop from disaster.

Simon stood up, put the laptop down on the table, then turned to face her, leaning back against the edge of the table, his arms crossed in front of him.

"What do you think you're trying to pull here?" Jo demanded.

"A deal," he said calmly. "So I won't

have to go to jail. It's my second offense for grand theft auto, after all."

"Don't give me that bull, Faro."

He seemed frustratingly undaunted by her ire. "Since we seem to be on a last-name basis, I should probably tell you I know your last name too, O'Neal." He had the gall to grin at her, a sexy grin. "Mary Jo O'Neal," he said reflectively, trying it out.

Jo felt something quiver inside her and took a firmer grip on herself. She couldn't afford to show any weakness. Not when it came to Simon Faro, his eyes giving away the direction of his thoughts, her own imagination supplying new and outrageous directions . . . no, she couldn't let it happen.

"What are you doing, making deals with my boss?"

"He was quite reasonable, if you want to know the truth."

"Reasonable? Since when do you find the chief *reasonable*?"

Simon's smile faded, growing a bit uncertain and vulnerable around the edges. Jo's heart gave a little squeeze. "Actually," Simon said. "I was desperate."

"Why? You knew I'd drop the charges."

"Yeah. That's what I was afraid of."

Jo's grip on her elbows loosened as she

stared at him, frowning, wary, scared of the inappropriate feelings churning inside her. "Afraid of?" she said in a small voice.

"Yeah. You'd drop the charges, put this whole case behind you, forget about it, and I'd never see you again. We don't exactly move in the same circles, Jo. I don't get arrested that often."

"That's right. We don't m-move in the same—"

He made an impatient gesture. "So I changed them. I changed the circles."

She shook her head. "I don't know what you're—"

"Yes, you do, Mary Jo. I'm talking about us. The two of us, together. I'm talking about what's been going on between us, underneath all this other stuff. The real truth."

His eyes had gone a darker, more intense gray that made her heart skip a little faster, that made her breath a little short. "Simon . . ."

"What?"

"I'm a . . . *cop*, Simon."

"Yeah. I know that."

"But you're not *acting* like you know it."

"What am I supposed to act like? You want me to call you *Detective*?"

"It wouldn't work, Simon! I mean—I give people traffic tickets!"

"I don't have a car anymore. I'm immune."

"You don't *like* cops! You think they're the bad guys."

"I don't think you're one of the bad guys, Jo."

"Give it a little time," she flung out, "and maybe you will. How long is it going to be before you decide I'm not free spirited enough or feminine enough, or . . ."

"Mary Jo . . ."

"Or sex—"

He closed the space between them with one long stride, pulled her against him with two strong hands, and brought his mouth down onto hers.

The kiss took her breath away. Not to mention her voice, her arguments, and her defenses. In Interrogation Room Two, of the Saratoga police headquarters, Simon Faro kissed her with enough heat to turn her blood to Saratoga Springs Vichy water. Her heart was racing when he lifted his head and met her gaze.

"Any woman who calls herself Cleopatra O'Nile is more than free spirited enough for me, Jo. And any woman who can wear a tablecloth and make me forget where I am and what I'm doing is feminine enough to be dangerous. And if you were any sexier, Mary Jo, I'd be dead by now."

She took in the words, afraid to believe them. Nonetheless, she felt a burst of joy that had no basis in fear.

"I know you're a cop, Mary Jo," he said. "I know what kind you are too. I know what you did to have Nickel's record cleared. Even more than that, I know that you will do whatever you can to make sure he goes in the right direction. I know you'll see that Nielson gets what he deserves, and you'll work damn hard to make sure it doesn't happen again in your department. That's what my story's going to be about. Maybe my next book. One good detective. One job well done. And you're going to come out looking like one hell of a good cop.

"And after hours, Mary Jo . . ." He moved closer to her, brushing their lips together, almost kissing her. "After hours, you're going to come out looking like one sexy, classy woman. One sexy, classy, ex-con's woman."

"Simon . . ." Her voice was breathy. "I don't know what to . . ."

"Mmm. You do." He nuzzled his mouth

against hers, teasing, tempting, urging her to open her lips to his kiss. "You don't have to decide right now. That was part of the deal with the chief, sweetcakes. A long engagement. As long as you like."

"Engagement? Simon . . ."

But what he was doing to her made the rest of the thought evaporate like August fog on Lake Saratoga. Moments later she slid her hands into his back pockets, pulling him closer.

Her fingers encountered an obstacle. Simon reached back to pull it out and toss it on the table beside the laptop. Jo's attention was momentarily distracted by the wad of bills that spilled across the metal surface. "Simon?"

"Mmm." He gave the money a quick glance. "It's yours, sweetcakes."

"Mine?"

"Venetian Red, in the sixth, to win. Paid off fifty-two to one. I had a hundred dollars on him."

"That's fifty-two hundred dollars?"

"Uh-huh. I thought," he added, pulling her toward him again, "we could spend it on the honeymoon."

She started to smile, feeling again that

expansive, joyful emotion burgeoning in her chest.

Love, she thought. That was what it was. Falling in love.

"Oh, yes, Simon. Let's do that."

"You see?" he murmured. "There's not a thing wrong with your instincts, Jo O'Neal. Not a single solitary thing."

THE EDITORS' CORNER

Passion and adventure reign in next month's LOVESWEPTs as irresistible heroes and unforgettable heroines find love under very unusual circumstances. When fate throws them together, it's only a matter of time before each couple discovers that danger can lead to desire. So get set to ward off the winter chill with these white-hot romances.

Helen Mittermeyer casts her spell again in **DIVINITY BROWN,** LOVESWEPT #782. They call him the black sheep of the county, a sexy ne'er-do-well who'd followed his own path—and found more than a little trouble. But when Jake Blessing comes asking for help from Divinity Brown, the curvy siren of a lawyer just can't say no! Helen Mittermeyer fashions an enthralling love story that transcends time.

Karen Leabo has long been popular with romance

readers for her fantastic love stories. So we're very pleased to present her Loveswept debut, **HELL ON WHEELS,** LOVESWEPT #783. A brash thrill-seeker who likes living on the edge isn't Victoria Holt's idea of the perfect partner for her annual tornado chase—but Roan Cullen is ready, willing, and hers! Roan revels in teasing the flame-haired meteorologist in the close quarters of the weather van, wondering if his fiery kisses can take this proper spitfire by storm. Will the forecast read: struck by lightning or love? Karen Leabo combines playful humor with sizzling sensuality in this fast-paced tale that you won't be able to put down.

Tensions run hot and steamy in Laura Taylor's **DANGEROUS SURRENDER,** LOVESWEPT #784. He'd thrown his body over hers as soon as gunfire erupted in the bank, but Carrie Forbes was shocked to feel passion mixed with fear when Brian York pulled her beneath him! The rugged entrepreneur tempts her as no man ever has, makes her crave what she thought she'd never know, but can she trust the sweet vows of intimacy when heartbreak still lingers in the shadow of her soul? Weaving a web of danger with the aphrodisiac of love on the run, Laura Taylor brilliantly explores the tantalizing threads that bind two strangers together.

Loveswept welcomes the talented Cynthia Powell, whose very first novel, **UNTAMED,** LOVESWEPT #785, rounds out this month's lineup in a very big way. "Don't move," a fierce voice commands—and Faline Eastbrook gasps at the bronzed warrior whose amber eyes sear her flesh! Brand Weston's gaze is bold, thrilling, and utterly uncivilized, but she can't let the "Wildman" see her tremble—not if she wants to capture his magnificent cats on film. Brand knows that staking his claim is reckless, but Faline has to be his. Cynthia Powell is the perfect writer for you if you love romance that's steamy, seductive, and more than a bit savage. Her sultry writing does no less than set the pages on fire!

Happy reading!

With warmest wishes,

Beth de Guzman

Senior Editor

Shauna Summers

Editor

P.S. Watch for these Bantam women's fiction titles coming in April: **MYSTIQUE,** Amanda Quick's latest bestseller, will be available in paperback. In nationally bestselling romances from RAINBOW to DEFIANT, Patricia Potter created stories that burn with the hot and dark emotions that bind a man and woman forever; now with **DIABLO,** this award-winning, highly acclaimed author sweeps readers once more into a breathtaking journey that transforms strangers into soulmates. Finally, from Geralyn Dawson comes **THE BAD LUCK WEDDING DRESS.** When her clients claim that wearing this dress is just asking for trouble, Jenny Fortune bets she can turn her luck around by wearing it at her own wedding. But first, she must find herself a groom! Be sure to see next month's LOVESWEPTs for a preview of these exceptional novels. And immediately following this page, preview the Bantam women's fiction titles on sale *now!*

Don't miss these extraordinary books
by your favorite Bantam authors

On sale in February:
GUILTY AS SIN
by *Tami Hoag*

BREATH OF MAGIC
by *Teresa Medeiros*

IVY SECRETS
by *Jean Stone*

Who can you trust?

Tami Hoag's impressive debut hardcover, NIGHT SINS, revealed her to be a masterful spinner of spine-chilling thrills. Now she once more tells a tale of dark suspense in . . .

GUILTY AS SIN

The kidnapping of eight-year-old Josh Kirkwood irrevocably altered the small town of Deer Lake, Minnesota. Even after the arrest of a suspect, fear maintains its grip and questions of innocence and guilt linger. Now, as Prosecutor Ellen North prepares to try her toughest case yet, she faces not only a sensation-driven press corps, political maneuvering, and her ex-lover as attorney for the defense, but an unwanted partner: Jay Butler Brooks, bestselling true-crime author and media darling, has been granted total access to the case—and to her. All the while, someone is following Ellen with deadly intent. When a second child is kidnapped while her prime suspect sits in jail, Ellen realizes that the game isn't over, it has just begun again. . . .

"If I were after you for nefarious purposes," he said as he advanced on Ellen, "would I be so careless as to approach you here?"

He pulled a gloved hand from his pocket and gestured gracefully to the parking lot, like a magician drawing attention to his stage.

"If I wanted to harm you," he said, stepping closer, "I would be smart enough to follow you home, find a way to slip into your house or garage, catch you where there would be little chance of witnesses or interference." He let those images take firm root in her mind. "That's what I would do if I were the sort of rascal who preys on women." He smiled again. "Which I am not."

"Who *are* you and what *do* you want?" Ellen demanded, unnerved by the fact that a part of her brain catalogued his manner as charming. No, not charming. Seductive. Disturbing.

"Jay Butler Brooks. I'm a writer—true crime. I can show you my driver's license if you'd like," he offered, but made no move to reach for it, only took another step toward her, never letting her get enough distance between them to diffuse the electric quality of the tension.

"I'd like for you to back off," Ellen said. She started to hold up a hand, a gesture meant to stop him in his tracks—or a foolish invitation for him to grab hold of her arm. Pulling the gesture back, she hefted her briefcase in her right hand, weighing its potential as a weapon or a shield. "If you think I'm getting close enough to you to look at a DMV photo, you must be out of your mind."

"Well, I have been so accused once or twice, but it never did stick. Now my Uncle Hooter, he's a different story. I could tell you some tales about him. Over dinner, perhaps?"

"Perhaps not."

He gave her a crestfallen look that was ruined by the sense that he was more amused than affronted. "After I waited for you out here in the cold?"

"After you stalked me and skulked around in the shadows?" she corrected him, moving another step backward. "After you've done your best to frighten me?"

"I frighten you, Ms. North? You don't strike me

as the sort of woman who would be easily frightened. That's certainly not the impression you gave at the press conference."

"I thought you said you aren't a reporter."

"No one at the courthouse ever asked," he confessed. "They assumed the same way you assumed. Forgive my pointing it out at this particular moment, but assumptions can be very dangerous things. Your boss needs to have a word with someone about security. This is a highly volatile case you've got here. Anything might happen. The possibilities are virtually endless. I'd be happy to discuss them with you. Over drinks," he suggested. "You look like you could do with one."

"If you want to see me, call my office."

"Oh, I want to see you, Ms. North," he murmured, his voice an almost tangible caress. "I'm not big on appointments, though. Preparation time eliminates spontaneity."

"That's the whole point."

"I prefer to catch people . . . off balance," he admitted. "They reveal more of their true selves."

"I have no intention of revealing anything to you." She stopped her retreat as a group of people emerged from the main doors of City Center. "I should have you arrested."

He arched a brow. "On what charge, Ms. North? Attempting to hold a conversation? Surely y'all are not so inhospitable as your weather here in Minnesota, are you?"

She gave him no answer. The voices of the people who had come out of the building rose and fell, only the odd word breaking clear as they made their way down the sidewalk. She turned and fell into step with the others as they passed.

Jay watched her walk away, head up, chin out, once again projecting an image of cool control. She didn't like being caught off guard. He would have bet money she was a list maker, a rule follower, the kind of woman who dotted all her *i*'s and crossed all her *t*'s, then double-checked them for good measure. She liked boundaries. She liked control. She had no intention of revealing anything to him.

"But you already have, Ms. Ellen North," he said, hunching up his shoulders as the wind bit a little harder and spat a sweep of fine white snow across the parking lot. "You already have."

From beloved national bestseller

Teresa Medeiros

comes an enchanting new time-travel romance

BREATH OF MAGIC

"Medeiros pens the ultimate romantic fantasy."
—Publishers Weekly

Arian Whitewood hadn't quite gotten the hang of the powerful amulet she'd inherited from her mother, but she never expected it to whisk her more than 300 years into the future. Flying unsteadily on her broomstick, she suddenly finds herself tumbling from the sky to land at the feet of Tristan Lennox. The reclusive Manhattan billionaire doesn't believe in magic, but he has his own reasons for offering one million dollars to anyone who can prove it exists.

Present-Day Manhattan

The media hadn't dubbed the four-thousand-square-foot penthouse perched at the apex of Lennox Tower "The Fortress" for nothing, Michael Copperfield thought as he changed elevators for the third time, keyed his security code into the lighted pad, and jabbed the button for the ninety-fifth floor.

The elevator doors slid open with a sibilant hiss. Resisting the temptation to gawk at the dazzling night view of the Manhattan skyline, Copperfield strode across a meadow of neutral beige carpet and shoved open the door at the far end of the suite.

"Do come in," said a dry voice. "Don't bother to knock."

Copperfield slapped that morning's edition of *The Times* on the chrome desk and stabbed a finger at the headline. "I just got back from Chicago. What in the hell is the meaning of this?"

A pair of frosty gray eyes flicked from the blinking cursor on the computer screen to the crumpled newspaper. "I should think it requires no explanation. You can't have been my PR advisor for all these years without learning how to read."

Copperfield glared at the man he had called friend for twenty-five years and employer for seven. "Oh, I can read quite well. Even between the lines." To prove his point, he snatched up the paper and read, " 'Tristan Lennox—founder, CEO, and primary stockholder of Lennox Enterprises—offers one million dollars to anyone who can prove that magic exists outside the boundaries of science. Public exhibition to be held tomorrow morning in the courtyard of Lennox Tower. Eccentric boy billionaire seeks only serious applicants.' " Copperfield twisted the paper as if to throttle his employer with it. "*Serious* applicants? Why, you'll have every psychic-hotline operator, swindler, and *Geraldo* reject on your doorstep by dawn!"

"Geraldo already called. I gave him your home number."

"How can you be so glib when I've faxed my fingers to the bone trying to establish a respectable reputation for you?"

Droll amusement glittered in Tristan's hooded eyes. "I'll give you a ten-thousand-dollar bonus if you can get them to stop calling me the 'boy billionaire.' It makes me feel like Bruce Wayne without the

Batmobile. And I did just turn thirty-two. I hardly qualify as a 'boy' anything."

"How long are you going to keep indulging these ridiculous whims of yours? Until you've completely destroyed your credibility? Until everyone in New York is laughing behind your back?"

"Until I find what I'm looking for."

"What? Or who?"

Ignoring Copperfield's pointed question, as he had for the past ten years, Tristan flipped off fax and computer with a single switch and rose from the swivel chair.

As he approached the north wall, an invisible seam widened to reveal a walk-in closet twice the size of Copperfield's loft apartment.

As Tristan activated an automated tie rack, Copperfield said, "Sometimes I think you flaunt convention deliberately. To keep everyone at arm's length where they can't hurt you." He drew in a steadying breath. "To keep the old scandal alive."

For a tense moment, the only sound was the mechanical swish of the ties circling their narrow track.

Then Tristan's shoulders lifted in a dispassionate shrug as he chose a burgundy striped silk to match his Armani suit. "Discrediting charlatans is a hobby. No different from playing the stock market or collecting Picassos." He knotted the tie with expert efficiency, shooting Copperfield a mocking glance. "Or romancing bulimic supermodels with Godiva chocolates."

Copperfield folded his arms over his chest. "Have you had my apartment under surveillance again, or did you conjure up that sordid image in your crystal ball? At least I give chocolates. As I recall, the last model I introduced you to didn't get so much as a 'thank you, ma'am' after her 'wham-bam.' "

Tristan's expression flickered with something that might have been shame in a less guarded man. "I meant to have my secretary send some flowers." He chose a pair of platinum cuff links from a mahogany tray. "If it's the million dollars you're worried about, Cop, don't waste your energy. I'm the last man who expects to forfeit that prize."

"Well, you know what they say. Within the chest of every cynic beats the heart of a disillusioned optimist."

Tristan brushed past him, fixing both his cuff links and his mask of aloof indifference firmly in place. "You should know better than anyone that I stopped believing in magic a long time ago."

"So you say, my friend," Copperfield murmured to himself. "So you say."

He pivoted only to discover that Tristan's exit had prompted the closet doors to glide soundlessly shut.

Copperfield rushed forward and began to bang on the seamless expanse with both fists. "Hey! Somebody let me out of here! Damn you, Tristan! You arrogant son of a—" A disbelieving bark of laughter escaped him as he braced his shoulder against the door. "Well, I'll be damned. What else can go wrong today?"

He found out an instant later when the mellow lighting programmed to respond solely to the mean average of his employer's heart rate flickered, then went out.

17th-Century Massachusetts

The girl plopped down on the broomstick. Her skirts bunched around her knees, baring a pair of slender calves shrouded in black stockings. A stray gust of wind rattled the dying leaves and ruffled her hair, forcing her to swipe a dark curl from her eyes. Gooseflesh prickled along her arms.

Shaking off the foreboding pall of the sky, she gripped the broomstick with both hands and screwed her eyes shut. As she attempted the freshly memorized words, a cramp shot down her thigh, shattering her concentration. She tried shouting the spell, but the broomstick did not deign to grant even a bored shudder in response.

Her voice faded to a defeated whisper. Disappointment swelled in her throat, constricting the tender membranes until tears stung her eyes. Perhaps she'd been deluding herself. Perhaps she was just as wretched a witch as she'd always feared.

She loosened the taut laces of her homespun bodice to toy with the emerald amulet suspended from a delicate filigree chain. Although she kept it well hidden from prying eyes and ignored its presence except in moments of dire vexation, she still felt compelled to wear it over her heart like a badge of shame.

"*Sacrébleu*, I only wanted to fly," she muttered.

The broomstick lurched forward, then jerked to a halt. The amulet lay cool and indifferent over her galloping heart.

Afraid to heed her own fickle senses, she slowly drew the gold chain over her head and squeezed the amulet. Leaning over the weather-beaten stick, she whispered, "I only wanted to fly."

Nothing.

She straightened, shaking her head at her own folly.

The willow broom sailed into the air and stopped, leaving her dangling by one leg. The stick quivered beneath her, the intensity of its power making the tiny hairs at her nape bristle with excitement.

"Fly!" she commanded with feeling.

The broom hung poised in midair for a shuddering eternity, then aimed itself toward the crowns of the towering oaks. It darted to a dizzying height, then swooped down, dragging her backside along the ground for several feet before shooting into another wild ascent.

She whooped in delight, refusing to consider the perils of soaring around a small clearing on a splintery hearth broom. The harder she laughed, the faster the broom traveled, until she feared it would surely bolt the clearing and shoot for the late-afternoon sky.

With a tremendous effort, she heaved herself astride the broom. She perched in relative comfort for a full heartbeat before the curious conveyance rocketed upward on a path parallel with the tallest oak, then dove downward with equal haste. The ground reached up to slam into her startled face.

She wheezed like a beached cod, praying the air would show mercy and fill her straining lungs. When she could finally breathe again, she lifted her throbbing head to find the broom lying a few feet away.

She spat out a mouthful of crumbled leaves and glared at the lifeless stick.

But her disgust was forgotten as she became aware of the gentle warmth suffusing her palm. She unfolded her trembling fingers to find the amulet bathed in a lambent glow. Her mouth fell open in wonder as the emerald winked twice as if to confirm their secret, then faded to darkness.

From the highly acclaimed author
of *First Loves* and *Sins of Innocence*

IVY SECRETS
by
Jean Stone

"Jean Stone understands the human heart."
—Literary Times

*With a poignant and evocative touch, Jean Stone tells the
enthralling story of three women from vastly different
backgrounds bound together by an inescapable lie. They
were roommates at one of New England's most prestigious
colleges; now Charlie, Tess, and Marina are haunted by the
truth of the past, and the fate of a young girl depends on
their willingness to tell . . . Ivy Secrets.*

She climbed the stairs to the fourth floor and slowly
went to her room. Inside, she sat on the edge of her
bed and let the tears flow quietly, the way a princess
had been taught. She hated the feeling that would not
go away, the feeling that there was another person
inside of her, wanting to spring out, wanting to be
part of the world. The world where people could talk
about their feelings, could share their hopes, their
dreams, their destinies not preordained. She hated
that her emotions were tangled with complications,
squeezed between oppressive layers of obligation, of
duty. Above it all, Marina longed for Viktor; she
ached for love. She held her stomach and bent for-

ward, trying to push the torment away, willing her tears to stop.

"Marina, what's wrong?"

Marina looked up. It was Charlie. And Tess.

"Nothing." She stood, wiped her tears. "I have a dreadful headache. And cramps." There was no way these two girls—blue-collar Charlie and odd, artsy Tess—would ever understand her life, her pain.

Tess walked into the room and sat at Marina's desk. "I hate cramps," she said. "My mother calls it the curse."

"I have a heating pad, Marina," Charlie said.

"Do you want some Midol?" Tess asked.

Marina slouched back on the bed. She could no longer hold back her tears. "It is not my period," she said. "It is Viktor."

Her friends were silent.

Marina put her face in her hands and wept. It hurt, it ached, it throbbed inside her heart. She had never—ever—cried in front of anyone. But as she tried to get control of herself, the sobs grew more intense. She struggled to stop crying. She could not.

Then she felt a hand on her shoulder. A gentle hand. "Marina?" Charlie asked. "What happened?"

Marina could not take her hands from her face.

"God, Marina," Tess said, "what did he do?"

She shook her head. "Nothing," she sobbed. "Absolutely nothing."

The girls were silent again.

"It's okay," Charlie said finally. "Whatever it is, it's okay. You can tell us."

"You'll feel better," Tess added. "Honest, you will."

Slowly, Marina's sobs eased. She sniffed for a moment, then set her hands on her lap. Through her watery eyes, she saw that Charlie sat beside her; Tess had moved her chair a little closer.

"He does not understand," she said. "He does not understand how much I love him." She stood and went to the window, not wanting to see their reactions. She yanked down the window shade. "There. I said it. I love Viktor Coe. I am in love with my damn bodyguard who doesn't give a rat's ass about me."

Charlie cleared her throat.

"Jesus," Tess said.

"I love him," Marina said. "And it is impossible. He is a bodyguard. I am a princess. Neither of you have any idea how that feels. You can fall in love with any boy you meet. It does not matter. The future of a country does not matter." She flopped back on the bed. Her limbs ached, her eyes ached, her heart felt as though it had been shattered into thousands of pieces.

"Does he know you love him?" Tess asked. "Have you told him?"

"There is no point. It would only cause more problems. Besides," she added as she hung her head. "He has someone else now. I have waited too long."

"He has someone else?" Charlie asked. "Here?"

"Yes," Marina said and cast a sharp glance at Tess. "Your friend, Tess. That woman. Dell Brooks."

Tess blinked. "Dell? God, she's my mother's age."

"Viktor is not much younger. He is in his thirties."

Tess blew out a puff of air. "Are you sure, Marina? I can't believe that Dell . . ."

"Believe it. I saw it with my own two eyes."

"Maybe they're just friends," Charlie said.

Marina laughed. "Americans are so naive."

"I think you should tell him," Tess said.

"I cannot."

"Yes, you can. The problem is, you won't."

Marina studied Tess. What could this teenage misfit possibly know? Or Charlie—the goody two-shoes who thought angora sweaters were the key to happiness?

"You won't tell him because you're afraid," Tess continued. "You're afraid he doesn't feel the same way about you, and then you'll be hurt."

"You sound like you know what you're talking about," Charlie said.

Tess shrugged. "It only makes sense. We may be naive Americans, but we know that hurt's part of life. Maybe Novokia-ites—or whatever you call yourselves —don't realize that."

Marina laughed. "I believe we are called Novoki-ans."

"Novokian, schmovokian. I think you should tell the man. Get it over with."

"You might be surprised at his reaction," Charlie agreed.

Marina looked at her closed shade. Viktor thought she was tucked in for the night, he thought she was safe. He had no idea that he was the one inflicting her pain, not the strangers that he anticipated were lurking behind every bush.

She turned to Charlie and Tess—her friends. This was, she reminded herself, part of why she had come to America. She had wanted friends. She had wanted to feel like a normal girl. Maybe Charlie and Tess were more "normal" than she'd thought. And maybe, just maybe, they were right.

"Will you help me?" Marina asked. "Will you help me figure out a plan?"

On sale in March:
MYSTIQUE
by Amanda Quick

DIABLO
by Patricia Potter

THE BAD LUCK WEDDING DRESS
by Geralyn Dawson

To enter the sweepstakes outlined below, you must respond by the date specified and follow all entry instructions published elsewhere in this offer.

DREAM COME TRUE SWEEPSTAKES

Sweepstakes begins 9/1/94, ends 1/15/96. To qualify for the Early Bird Prize, entry must be received by the date specified elsewhere in this offer. Winners will be selected in random drawings on 2/29/96 by an independent judging organization whose decisions are final. Early Bird winner will be selected in a separate drawing from among all qualifying entries.

Odds of winning determined by total number of entries received. Distribution not to exceed 300 million.

Estimated maximum retail value of prizes: Grand (1) $25,000 (cash alternative $20,000); First (1) $2,000; Second (1) $750; Third (50) $75; Fourth (1,000) $50; Early Bird (1) $5,000. Total prize value: $86,500.

Automobile and travel trailer must be picked up at a local dealer; all other merchandise prizes will be shipped to winners. Awarding of any prize to a minor will require written permission of parent/guardian. If a trip prize is won by a minor, s/he must be accompanied by parent/legal guardian. Trip prizes subject to availability and must be completed within 12 months of date awarded. Blackout dates may apply. Early Bird trip is on a space available basis and does not include port charges, gratuities, optional shore excursions and onboard personal purchases. Prizes are not transferable or redeemable for cash except as specified. No substitution for prizes except as necessary due to unavailability. Travel trailer and/or automobile license and registration fees are winners' responsibility as are any other incidental expenses not specified herein.

Early Bird Prize may not be offered in some presentations of this sweepstakes. Grand through third prize winners will have the option of selecting any prize offered at level won. All prizes will be awarded. Drawing will be held at 204 Center Square Road, Bridgeport, NJ 08014. Winners need not be present. For winners list (available in June, 1996), send a self-addressed, stamped envelope by 1/15/96 to: Dream Come True Winners, P.O. Box 572, Gibbstown, NJ 08027.

THE FOLLOWING APPLIES TO THE SWEEPSTAKES ABOVE:

No purchase necessary. No photocopied or mechanically reproduced entries will be accepted. Not responsible for lost, late, misdirected, damaged, incomplete, illegible, or postage-die mail. Entries become the property of sponsors and will not be returned.

Winner(s) will be notified by mail. Winner(s) may be required to sign and return an affidavit of eligibility/release within 14 days of date on notification or an alternate may be selected. Except where prohibited by law, entry constitutes permission to use of winners' names, hometowns, and likenesses for publicity without additional compensation. Void where prohibited or restricted. All federal, state, provincial, and local laws and regulations apply.

All prize values are in U.S. currency. Presentation of prizes may vary; values at a given prize level will be approximately the same. All taxes are winners' responsibility.

Canadian residents, in order to win, must first correctly answer a time-limited skill testing question administered by mail. Any litigation regarding the conduct and awarding of a prize in this publicity contest by a resident of the province of Quebec may be submitted to the Regie des loteries et courses du Quebec.

Sweepstakes is open to legal residents of the U.S., Canada, and Europe (in those areas where made available) who have received this offer.

Sweepstakes in sponsored by Ventura Associates, 1211 Avenue of the Americas, New York, NY 10036 and presented by independent businesses. Employees of these, their advertising agencies and promotional companies involved in this promotion, and their immediate families, agents, successors, and assignees shall be ineligible to participate in the promotion and shall not be eligible for any prizes covered herein.   SWP 3/95

DON'T MISS THESE FABULOUS
BANTAM WOMEN'S FICTION TITLES

On Sale in March

MYSTIQUE

from *New York Times* bestseller Amanda Quick
in paperback ____ 57159-1 $6.50/$7.99 in Canada

DIABLO

by *Romantic Times's* Storyteller of the Year
Patricia Potter

Nicky Thompson can hold her own with outlaws, but nothing in her experience has prepared her for the new brand of danger named Diablo. ____ 56602-4 $5.50/$7.50 in Canada

THE BAD LUCK WEDDING DRESS

by ever-talented Geralyn Dawson
"One of the best new authors to come along in years
—fresh, charming, and romantic."
—*New York Times* bestselling author Jill Barnett

When her clients claim that wearing this dress is just asking for trouble, Fortune Davenport bets she can turn her luck around by wearing it at her own wedding. But first she must find herself a groom. . . . ____ 56792-6 $4.99/$6.99 in Canada

----

Ask for these books at your local bookstore or use this page to order.

Please send me the books I have checked above. I am enclosing $____ (add $2.50 to cover postage and handling). Send check or money order, no cash or C.O.D.'s, please.

Name _____

Address _____

City/State/Zip _____

Send order to: Bantam Books, Dept. FN159, 2451 S. Wolf Rd., Des Plaines, IL 60018
Allow four to six weeks for delivery.

Prices and availability subject to change without notice. FN 159 3/96